I surveyed the pile of debris: chunks of broken plaster, bricks, laths. The studs had held. A coating of plaster grit covered everything, including us.

And then something caught my eye. A smooth rounded shape that didn't fit, yet seemed inexplicably familiar. There was something about it.

I pulled heavy gloves out of my back pocket and slipped them on. With my gloved hands I dug around the object, freeing it. I had to use both hands to lift it out of the rubble, and I stood for a moment gaping at my discovery, my brain disbelieving what my eyes were seeing.

A skull. I was holding a human skull.

★

Previously published Worldwide Mystery titles by
ELLEN ELIZABETH HUNTER

MURDER ON THE CANDLELIGHT TOUR
MURDER AT THE AZALEA FESTIVAL
MURDER AT WRIGHTSVILLE BEACH
MURDER ON THE ICW

Ellen Elizabeth Hunter

MURDER ON THE GHOST WALK

TORONTO • NEW YORK • LONDON
AMSTERDAM • PARIS • SYDNEY • HAMBURG
STOCKHOLM • ATHENS • TOKYO • MILAN
MADRID • WARSAW • BUDAPEST • AUCKLAND

Recycling programs
for this product may
not exist in your area.

MURDER ON THE GHOST WALK

A Worldwide Mystery/December 2009

First published by Magnolia Mysteries.

ISBN-13: 978-0-373-26693-7

Printed in U.S.A.

Acknowledgments

The historic district of Wilmington and the Ghost Walk tour inspired me to write this book. The Historic District's peaceful, shady streets and elegant old mansions are populated with otherworldly spirits— or so the folklore goes. I have taken literary liberties with the geography of Orange Street, but I trust I have captured the charm and beauty of that street.

A special thank-you to Beverly Tetterton, Special Collections Librarian, North Carolina Room, New Hanover County Public Library, for reading my manuscript with an eye toward historical accuracy.

Hugs to the Cape Fear Crime Festival's board members who agreed to "play" themselves in cameo roles.

And thanks to John Hirchak and the guides of the Ghost Walk tour. The tour is spooky and a bit unnerving; still I recommend it highly.

As always, kudos to Tim Doby who designs my books; he is an artist first, a graphics designer second.

I tried to get things right, and to be respectful of Wilmington, her citizens and history.

ONE

SUNSHINE DAPPLED the deck of The Pilot House Restaurant, warming my shoulders. Early morning fog, so prevalent in October, had lifted hours ago and the afternoon was mellowing with incredible beauty. The entire East Coast was in the thrall of a fine Indian summer. Sunbeams sparkled off the Cape Fear River as it flowed swiftly beneath my feet. Downstream, Memorial Bridge sang with traffic. I could feel my spirits lift, as if the macabre events of the morning had not happened to me—had not happened at all.

I looked up to see my beautiful sister step through the restaurant's rear door and out onto the deck. Melanie is eight years older than I, thirty-two to my twenty-four. She has a way of making an entrance, of commanding a room. Gracefully, she glided among the tables. Heads turned, eyes admired.

With a practiced hand, she flipped her shoulder-length auburn hair. Melanie inherited the fashion genes in our family. Her apricot sweater set complimented her coloring and her brown Capri pants showed off her long legs. She fluttered her fingers my way while nodding to other diners. Melanie is Wilmington's star Realtor, and she had risen to that position by working hard and building friendships.

"Hey, shug," she greeted. She bent to kiss my cheek. I was glad I'd stopped in the restaurant's pretty yellow ladies' room to wash my face and comb the plaster dust out of my hair.

"Have you heard? It must be on the news," I said.

She dropped her Holly Golightly sunglasses onto the umbrella-shaded tabletop and sat down. Reaching for a menu, she said, "The news? You know I don't listen to that gloom and doom stuff. I've been out at Wrightsville Beach all morning, showing houses to a couple from Raleigh."

She looked me over from head to toe with the same severe scrutiny the homicide detective had subjected me to. "Was there an accident? Are you all right?" Her yellow-green eyes narrowed as she inspected me closely. "Have you been crying? Your eyes are all red."

I swallowed a gulp of sugary iced tea. "Just dirt from the site, is all." I took a deep breath, about to launch into my narrative when the waitress approached and asked for our orders. "Carolina shrimp bisque," I said, then added, "And bring a basket of dinner rolls, would you please." I have a bad habit of overeating when life turns stressful. Consequently, I am always battling the extra pounds.

Melanie ordered a salad, low-fat dressing on the side.

"So what happened?" she said to me, "Oh, shoot…" She lifted one perfectly manicured finger, requesting patience. From inside her Kelly bag, her cell phone played an electronic version of *Carolina Moon*.

"Sorry, shug," she said, "I've got to take this. I stood someone up to meet you."

I listened as she explained that her baby sister had an

emergency. I tuned out the darlin's and sugah's as she sweet-talked her client or new boyfriend—or could they be one and the same? A bread basket appeared magically and I slathered butter on scrumptious corn bread.

My gaze played over the river as the sweet corn bread melted in my mouth. I'm home, I told myself, home for good. After four years of a shared, cramped Big Apple apartment, followed by two years of camping with Aunt Ruby in Savannah, I'd come home to hang out my shingle, *Historic Restorations by Ashley*. And to live in a snug bungalow of my own. If I ever leave Wilmington again, I vowed, it will be feet first.

At age eighteen, I had done the unthinkable, something no Wilkes or Chastain had ever dreamt of doing: I'd moved to New York City. Mama had been horrified, convinced I'd be ravished while waiting for the "walk" light in front of Saks. Daddy had taken me quietly aside to assure me he had sufficient faith in what he called my "good common horse sense" to trust me to live in the big city while I pursued a Bachelor of Fine Arts from Parsons School of Design, my dream since I opened my first box of 64 Crayolas with sharpener. "But if you ever want to come home," he had said, "all you have to do is pick up the phone. I'll be there to collect you in a New York minute." A promise he would not be able to keep.

That first Christmas when I returned to our home on Summer Rest Road had turned out to be the saddest holiday of my life. On Christmas Eve, Daddy—Judge Peter Wilkes—left our house to retrieve a forgotten file at the court house. He never returned. He died in the ambulance after driving into one of the largest Live Oak trees on Airlie Drive, just outside Airlie Gardens—a tree that might have been planted by Mrs. Pembroke Jones herself. I knew Daddy had been dipping into the spiced eggnog all afternoon, but he had seemed perfectly sober when I waved him out of the driveway.

After an appropriate interval of formal mourning, I returned to Parsons to attack school projects with a vengeance, and four years later graduated at the top of my class. Mama's family, the Chastains, were an old Savannah family. I enrolled in the Masters program in Historic Preservation at SCAD, the Savannah College of Art and Design, and lived with my Aunt Ruby in the family home for two years. Old Savannah with its Queen Anne and Italianate style homes had been my classroom.

I TUNED OUT Melanie as she skillfully managed her caller and felt a warm cozy glow because we were together again. Absently, she twirled a silky strand of auburn hair around her finger. Her face was creamy ivory, a perfect oval, just like Mama's.

How I had worshiped my big sister when we were growing up. Melanie was everything I wanted to be: pretty and popular, outgoing and smart. I always felt like I'd never catch up. I had turned to art, filling my sketch pad with castles and cottages, gabled roofs and rose-covered picket fences. I excelled in art classes. Melanie excelled in life. Everything she touched turned to gold. And, oh, the men she'd had.

Which led me to thoughts of the handsome detective

I'd met just hours earlier. Nicholas Yost. I wondered if he was single. I hadn't seen a wedding ring on his finger, but that was no guarantee.

Then the full horror of the morning's events came streaming back and even with the sun beating down on top of my head, I shivered, thinking of the mayhem that must have occurred in that once glorious mansion. I wanted my big sister to get off the phone and hug me, to tell me everything was going to be all right. Someone had killed those people, someone I might even know.

TWO

THAT MORNING HAD BEGUN like any other day in the past two weeks since we'd begun restoring the Campbell mansion. I parked my mother's station wagon at the curb on Orange Street behind Willie Hudson's row of trucks and Jon Campbell's Jeep.

The mansion rose before me on the other side of an ornate wrought iron fence. In 1840 it had been as impressive as the large, elegant mansions of Williamsburg, and I suspect that is what Reginald Campbell, the original owner, had in mind when he'd had it built. In those days, the house would have symbolized a standard of great wealth; it would have proclaimed to one and all that a man of substance lived behind its solid, thick brick walls.

The house was Federal in style with double-hung sash windows arranged symmetrically around a center entrance. The windows were framed with louvered shutters. The semicircular Greek Revival portico sported a crown-like roof and decorative columns. An imposing archway surrounded the front door. Rising two stories high, the house was sheltered by a low-pitched roof with a balustrade. It was a magnificent example of late-Federal architecture.

But Campbell House was now in very bad shape. Mortar crumbled between the bricks, leaving gaping holes; the trim paint was blistered and peeling. One of the second floor window panes had been pierced, shards of glass radiating from a small round hole. Inside, things were worse.

The wrought iron gate was propped open with a brick. I had been about to step through it when someone called, "Miss! Miss!" I turned to see a tiny woman with permed gray hair waving to me from the front porch of the cottage across the street. "Wait," she cried and descended the steps cautiously, crossed her lawn, then shuffled across the street.

"Mercy," she panted as she reached my side, one hand pressed over her heart.

"Are you OK, ma'am?"

Her gray head bobbed up and down. "Just let me catch my breath."

I studied her face. Good bones supported thin skin well. Her eyes were blue. I suspected that once they had been bright blue but now they were faded. Still they were lively and sharp.

"I'm Ellen Burns from across the street." She pointed with her chin to a small white clapboard coastal cottage with a broad front porch.

"Ashley Wilkes," I said, extending my hand. Clasping her hand in mine was like catching a bony trembling bird.

"You're remodeling their house," she said. "Does that mean they're coming home?"

I gazed up at the house while puzzling over her question. I'd learned from Melanie that the previous owners had moved abroad. "Do you mean Reggie and Shelby Campbell?" I asked.

"You have to turn this way so I can read your lips," Mrs. Burns told me. "My hearing is not what it used to be. Now what did you say?"

I repeated my question and noticed that she studied my lips intently.

"Yes," she replied softly. "Reggie and Shelby Campbell. Reggie's mother, Jean, was my best friend before she passed. That was seven years ago. I still miss her. We were like this." She crossed two fingers.

"I'm sorry," I said, wondering why she was confiding in me.

"But then after she was gone, Reggie and Shelby became my friends as well. I have trouble sleeping, you see. And Reggie and Shelby are night owls, so we'd get together and play cards some nights."

"I heard they bought a villa in Tuscany," I commented.

"Yes," she said thoughtfully, "that's what I heard too."

"I'm not restoring this house for them. It's been sold."

She looked up at the decaying mansion and a worried expression crossed her face. "I saw them leave that night. I waved, but they didn't wave back."

She seemed saddened by this memory, as if the slight still smarted. "They didn't tell me they were leaving. But then that was just like them. Goodness me, they were impulsive folks. Here one day, gone the next. But how long can you traipse around the world and not get homesick?"

I didn't know how to respond. "I only met them once," I commented. "At their Christmas ball seven years ago."

"Oh, yes. That was shortly after Jean died. I remember because they struggled over the decision of whether to cancel the party. But the community was used to it, you see, expected it. And as it turned out, it was their last party. Now we've been waiting for years for them to come home and throw another Christmas ball." She sighed wistfully.

Then, suddenly energized, she seized my arm with both hands. "Jean is watching for them. She started playing the organ right after they left. I used to hear it at night when I couldn't sleep."

I must have looked startled because she explained, "Something as loud as an organ, even I can hear."

But that was not what had startled me. I'd heard rumors of a ghost organist but I refused to buy into the supernatural. "I'd better check on the work inside," I said. "It was nice to meet you, Mrs. Burns."

She stared at the house, clearly disappointed. "So you're not working for Shelby and Reggie?"

"I'm afraid not, Mrs. Burns. I work for the new owner, Mirabelle Morgan. Perhaps you've seen her on television. She has that cooking show, *Southern Style*."

Ellen Burns flapped a frail hand in front of her face. "Oh, her? She owns the house now? That phony! And she's going to live here? Ah, Jean will surely be rid of her in short order." She smiled as if the thought was the most fun she'd had in weeks, before shuffling off to return to her cottage.

I HURRIED UP the sidewalk and let myself in. The broad formal reception hall ran straight through to the back of the house, telescoping into a rear hallway with a back door that exited into an overgrown garden. On my right, a wide staircase curved gently upward to the second floor. Beyond the staircase, just past the door under the stairs that led to the basement, heavy gauge vinyl sheeting had been hung, sealing off the kitchen area from the front rooms.

On my left lay a large formal double parlor. On my right was the dining room, with a butler's pantry beyond it that connected to the kitchen wing. Vinyl sheeting hung there as well.

Signs of neglect were visible everywhere, from the accumulated dust on the abandoned antiques to evidence of rodents tunneling into the heart pine floors. Dampness had set in and the dining room's elegant silk wallpaper had loosened and sagged. Pastel paint on the walls in other rooms was streaked with mildew. Cobwebs filled every corner.

Six years is a long time for a house to be locked up and abandoned. And Wilmington's humid climate accelerated decay.

I lifted a flap in the vinyl sheeting, entered the rear hallway, and stepped through a doorway into the kitchen. Here, the air was chalky with plaster dust. Early nineteenth century plaster was a mixture of ground oyster shells, sand, and hog or cattle hair, all of which had been readily available in our coastal community in the early eighteen hundreds. In a fine house like this, marble dust might have been added to the last coat of plaster to give it a hard-finish white sheen, but only in the formal rooms. Here, in the kitchen, the walls had been painted and repainted many times.

Architect Jon Campbell was directing the strip-out phase, although Willie Hudson, our general contractor, did not need supervision. Willie was a sixty-something general contractor who knew more about old house construction than Jon and I put together. His crew consisted of sons, grandsons, and nephews, all thoroughly trained by himself.

I looked up to where the twelve foot wall joined the ceiling. This was the wall we were demolishing. Already the plaster had been stripped, exposing the laths beneath. Laths are narrow strips of wood furring that are nailed to the studs horizontally to provide a surface for plaster.

Curtis, one of Willie Hudson's grandsons was up on a ladder, grasping one end of a steel beam that would be wedged atop upright studs, snugged up under the ceiling to act as a temporary header while we removed the wall. This was not a load-bearing wall so theoretically we did not need a header, but you never take chances with old house construction because it offered too many opportunities for surprises.

Curtis's cousin, Dwayne, was climbing the second ladder, lugging up the opposite end of the steel beam. They were joking as they usually did, laughing over some private joke, when Dwayne lost his footing. His arms flailed wildly as he tried to regain his balance, and the beam slipped out of his grasp.

Curtis cried out loudly as he struggled to hold on to his end. The loose end of the beam went flying, crashing against the wall with a shattering force. It broke through ancient, brittle laths, then rebounded as if it had a will of its own, falling straight for us.

"Move!" I cried.

Dwayne and Curtis, young and agile, jumped clear of the ladders. But Willie, whose reflexes were slow, did not move fast enough. I grabbed his arm and jerked him away from danger as Jon scrambled off to the side.

All this took place in the blink of an eye, yet at the same time the accident seemed to progress in slow motion.

A large gaping hole appeared where the beam had struck the laths. Dry, crumbling scratch plaster and loose bricks spilled out of the interior like sand out of a chute. When the wall stopped quaking, when everything that was going to fall had fallen, we looked about assessing the damage.

"No one's hurt, at least," I said.

"And that wall is coming down anyway," Jon said, "so no harm done."

We heaved a collective sigh of relief; it could have been worse.

The restoration period is the most vulnerable time for a structure, and strip-out is one of the most dangerous periods. If an accident is going to happen it usually happens then, no matter how well the design is planned, nor how prudently the demolition team works.

I surveyed the pile of debris: chunks of broken plaster, bricks, laths. The studs had held. A coating of plaster grit covered everything, including us.

And then something caught my eye. A smooth rounded shape that didn't fit, yet seemed inexplicably familiar. There was something about it.

I pulled heavy gloves out of my back pocket and slipped them on. With my gloved hands I dug around the object, freeing it. I had to use both hands to lift it out of the rubble, and I stood for a moment gaping at my discovery, my brain disbelieving what my eyes were seeing.

A skull. I was holding a human skull.

THREE

WITHIN MINUTES the house was overrun with uniformed police officers and firefighters.

Then the detectives arrived. The detective in charge was a man of about thirty who introduced himself as Detective Nicholas Yost. He surveyed the demolition area, asked surprisingly intelligent questions, and within minutes owned the crime scene.

Circling around the kitchen space, he stopped before me and studied me with such intensity I became embarrassingly aware of how I must look to the perfectly groomed detective.

My dark curls were mashed down and damp from my hard hat. My construction boots were chalky and at their best are not very feminine looking. My khaki shorts and denim shirt were dusty. I ran my fingers through my hair, trying to lift it off my forehead, but only succeeded in transferring dirt there too.

The detective's eyes crinkled at the corners, but he only said in a crisp, professional tone, "Let's step out here where we can talk," and led the way through the vinyl sheeting and into the reception hall. He asked my name, his notepad and pen poised. When I replied Ashley Wilkes, he gave me a searching look. "I believe

I knew your father. Judge Wilkes was your father, wasn't he?"

"Yes," I said softly.

"Good man. We miss him."

Maybe it was a delayed reaction to the shock of finding that skull, but my eyes filled with tears. I blinked them back, not wanting to make a fool of myself in front of this stranger. Just the mention of my father reminded me of how I'd always relied on him in tough situations. If he were alive, I'd be on the phone with him right now, and he'd be saying, "Hang on, sweetheart, I'll be right there."

"I miss him too," I said softly, surprised that I was sharing my tender feelings with a hard-boiled detective. Except that he wasn't hard-boiled. Behind the guarded expression, the cocky posturing, compassion flowed from him to me. *This is a good guy,* I realized with a flash of intuition.

Anxiety must have shown on my face because he reached out a hand to steady me. "You've had a nasty shock, Miss Wilkes. Here, sit down."

He motioned to two shield-back Hepplewhite side chairs that I intended to send out for cleaning, and we sat in them. He watched me, his gaze controlled, yet I detected male-female interest. He liked me, even I could see that. His eyes were a beautiful hazel, his face a long oval, moderately tan, and his light ash-brown hair was neatly combed to the side. "Your dad was one of the best judges we ever had in New Hanover County."

I brushed a watery eye with the back of my hand,

smearing dust into it and causing it to tear. I tried to eliminate the irritant by blinking rapidly.

Detective Yost pulled a packet of tissues out of his jacket pocket and handed them to me. "Look, Miss Wilkes, you're upset and I don't blame you. It was hard on you, finding that skull. Just give me your address and telephone number and you can go. I'll contact you later for a statement." He stood up, our interview over.

I gave him my address on Summer Rest Road. He snapped the notebook shut and slipped it into his inside jacket pocket. With his jacket open, I saw how fit he was, how well-dressed, how costly his suit must have been. I also glimpsed a shoulder holster and an impressive piece of weaponry. I don't know one gun from another but this was heavy-duty, obviously police-issue. The sight of that gun brought home the gravity of my situation: I'd stumbled into a homicide case. Someone had killed that person in the wall.

"You OK? You want an officer to drive you home?" Yost took my elbow and helped me to stand.

"I'll be all right," I replied. "But thanks for the offer."

"What is your role here?" he asked.

"I'm a historic preservationist," I explained. "I oversee the project, kind of a site supervisor. I do a lot of the design work. I file the Certificate of Appropriateness with the historic commission, see that we adhere to the guidelines, keep us legal."

He nodded. "I handled some of the paperwork when my dad and I remodeled our house. Must be pretty complicated with a house this important. Well, you take care of yourself, Miss Wilkes. I wouldn't want anything happening to Judge Wilkes's daughter."

He smiled at me and I was surprised to see dimples appear on either side of his mouth. I fought the urge to reach out and touch them. Unaware of how his smile affected me, he gave me a polite nod and stepped briskly toward the kitchen wing.

I found myself thinking that since he had my phone number, maybe he'd call. Then I gave myself a shake, admonishing myself that I was involved with a police investigation not a dating service.

I was making my way out when an entourage of officials hurried through the open door and swept me back inside with them. Uniformed cops and forensic technicians surrounded a tall, distinguished-looking man, whom they all seemed to defer to. One of the cops called him Dr. Banks. *The medical examiner,* I realized. They filed through the flap in the vinyl sheeting and disappeared into the kitchen wing, leaving me alone in the hall again.

Curiosity got the better of me and I went through the dining room and into the butler's pantry to spy on them. Concealed by the frosty vinyl, I withdrew a pocketknife from my shorts and carved a small window in the sheeting.

They were all in there, combing through the debris. I watched the scene unfold for as long as my stomach could take it. Dr. Banks cupped the skull in his gloved hands, holding it almost reverently. I swallowed hard. Then the forensic technicians began handing him bones which he arranged on a large tarp they'd spread out over the plaster-littered floor. A man and a woman, he said. My stomach rebelled, and I fled back through the reception hall and out the front door. Fresh air. I gulped it.

A crowd had gathered on the sidewalk, pushing up against the wrought iron fence. A lone uniformed officer guarded the gate which was now closed. Orange Street looked like a disaster site, emergency vehicles and police cars parked every which way, their lights throbbing, their radios barking.

Across the street, Mrs. Burns watched from her front porch, one arm wrapped around a post for support.

"Ashley!" a familiar voice called.

I scanned the faces in the crowd and spotted Binkie. The officer opened the gate for me and let me out. I pushed through the crowd to join Binkie at the curb. His little band of tourists surrounded him. They had set out on the Ghost Walk tour and ended up at a murder scene.

Several years ago, Sherman and Muffie Warner, the couple who lived in the Italianate house on the corner, had complained of hearing organ music at night. The rumors that Campbell House was haunted by a ghost organist spread through the town. An Aeolian pipe organ, dating from about 1910, filled one wall of the ballroom on the second floor. I'd heard Jean Campbell play it on a long ago Christmas tour.

"Ashley?" Binkie cried. "What has happened? The police won't tell us anything except that it's police business. Are you all right? Someone said a wall collapsed. Let me take you to your car where you can sit down."

Binkie instructed his tour group to wait and he took my arm and we bucked the crowd to my car. Once inside, I realized there was no way I would be able to drive away. My station wagon was blocked by a fire truck.

With Binkie beside me, patting my shoulder and telling me to take deep breaths, to put my head between my knees if I felt faint, I began to relax. He smiled, his fair skin crinkling, his seventy-year-old blue eyes as bright and keen as if they belonged to a seventeen-year-old. He had on a moss green felt hat with a jaunty little brown speckled feather. His favorite brown and cream herringbone tweed jacket was holding up well despite constant wearing. Brown corduroy slacks looked soft and comfortable, as did his brown suede Hush Puppies.

Binkie is a Professor Emeritus at UNCW's History Department. No one knows more about the history and folklore of the Lower Cape Fear region. He has authored many scholarly books on the subject. With his friends—with everyone—he is kindly and gracious, a Southern gentleman of the old school. I had moments when I wished I were a handsome seventy-year-old matron so we could fall in love.

As if reading my mind—and sometimes he does—he reached out and cradled my hand in both of his. His hands were worn like everything else about him, but offered reassurance and comfort. After Daddy died, Binkie stepped into my life and I leaned on him. He seemed to need someone to need him, for he had never married and had no family. We'd gotten together every time I came home on a school break.

With tears welling in my eyes, I blurted out the whole story of the accident, finding the skull, and how the medical examiner discovered the bones of two bodies.

"Oh, I knew it," he exclaimed. "I knew something dreadful had happened here. Your discovery explains why this house has been the site of so many disturbances these past several years. Places have spirits too, you know; I've sensed that the spirit of this house was grieving."

"You really believe that, don't you?"

He squeezed my hand. "There is much that is unseen by humankind, Ashley dear. The more we discover, the more we realize how much there remains to be discovered."

He patted my hand and let it go. "Now, I think you should call Melanie. She won't be able to drive her car into this horrific traffic jam, but perhaps she can meet you somewhere nearby for lunch, then take you home. Don't even think of going back to your studio. Now, would you like me to escort you to the riverfront? I must shepherd my little flock there."

AND SO MY SISTER Melanie had driven in from the beach to meet me at The Pilot House Restaurant. Now she dropped her phone in her purse and said, "Sorry about that, sweetie. Business, you know. Now tell me everything."

Quickly, I began my chronicle of the morning's events, told her how a portion of the interior wall had collapsed.

"But you're not hurt," she cried.

I assured her I was only dirty. And unnerved.

Just then our food came and I practically inhaled the

shrimp bisque. Hot, spicy, creamy shellfish stew. Coastal comfort food. In between swallows, I described finding the skull, and how law enforcement had arrived in full force.

When I got to the part about Dr. Banks saying there were two skeletons, a man and a woman, the fork fell from her grasp and her golden green eyes popped wide.

"Shut up!" she declared. "Two skeletons! There were two skeletons?"

"Yes, two. I hung around and watched him count the bones: four femurs, four tibias. The two skulls were a dead giveaway." I giggled uncontrollably.

"You've had a nasty shock, baby sister. Here, drink your tea, the sugar and caffeine will do you good." She got subdued, face grave, eyes downcast. "Shelby and Reggie. It's got to be them."

"Shelby and Reggie? But how can that be? They gave you the listing on the mansion and you sold it to Mirabelle. More likely a couple of drifters broke into the house."

"And climbed inside a wall to die like old sick cats? Get real. It has to be them."

"But aren't they on some tour?" I protested. "Everyone says they were buying a house in Italy."

"But this is home. Surely they would have come back, if only to settle their affairs here."

"So someone made up that story. I never understood how they could abandon that beautiful house."

She picked up her fork again and stabbed a lettuce leaf. "Well, now we know they didn't. They've been here all along."

I stared at the river blindly, seeing something else. "Shelby Campbell did have long blonde hair, didn't she?"

Melanie narrowed her eyes suspiciously. "Yes. Down to her tush. What are you getting at?"

"There was a hank of something that I thought was straw. But it was hair. Dried out yellow hair."

Melanie pushed her plate aside. "Well, that does it. I cannot eat another bite. Oh, yuck. How distasteful."

"But, Mel, I don't understand. How could those skeletons be Reggie and Shelby when they gave you the listing to sell their house for them?"

She sniffed, then leaned across the table to confide, "That's not how it happened. I bought the house from the city. At foreclosure."

Well, that explained her new Lexus RX300. I knew the monstrous sum Mirabelle had paid for that house.

"Is that legal?" I asked.

"Absolutely legal," she said flatly. "In fact I did the city a favor. The taxes hadn't been paid in years. The house was attracting vagrants and the county commissioners were getting complaints. No one could find the Campbells. Funny thing, though. Reggie and Shelby left—that is, disappeared—six years ago but the property taxes were paid for the first three years of their absence."

"So that means they were alive for those first three years. Or…someone else was paying the taxes. Oh, it was the killer. The killer paid the taxes!"

I flopped back in my chair. "I remember how sweet they were to me that time we went to their Christmas ball. I wish someone else had found them." I threw my napkin on the table and dropped my head into my hands.

Melanie scooted her chair close to mine and cradled me in her arms. "There, there, shug. Don't cry. It's going to be all right. You'll see."

FOUR

AFTER LUNCH, I strolled across cobblestoned Chandler's Wharf to my small studio to play back my telephone messages. And, yes, there were many. Every television and print reporter in the county and as far away as Charlotte and Raleigh wanted to talk to me about finding the skeletons. One message was from Mirabelle. No mistaking that autocratic tone. She'd been treating me like her personal servant since day one.

"I'm flying in from New York this afternoon, sweetie," the message said. "My plane lands at four. I need you to pick me up at the airport. Meet me right outside security. Oh, and Ashley, you know I don't like to be kept waiting."

No "please." No "thank you." Just another instruction issued, as if she were selecting paint colors. One glance at my watch and I realized her plane was airborne; no way could I reach her to warn her.

I trudged up the hill to the Campbell mansion for my car. The emergency vehicles were gone. So were Willie Hudson's trucks and Jon's Jeep. But the medical examiner's van, the Crime Scene Unit, and two blue-and-white Wilmington P.D. cruisers were parked on the street. Yellow crime scene tape cordoned off the property. Most of the crowd had given up and left. Ellen Burns sat on her porch. I gave her a wave as I got into my car, then drove home for a much-needed shower and change of clothes.

Arriving at Wilmington International Airport, I discovered that Mirabelle's flight was delayed, a common occurrence in these days of high security. I settled down to wait, my thoughts drifting back to the first time I met Mirabelle. I had been seventeen, a senior in high school, and feeling so grown up to be attending Reggie and Shelby Campbell's annual Christmas ball. Parsons had just accepted my application; I knew what I wanted to do with the rest of my life.

The Campbell residence was one of the few homes in Wilmington with its own ballroom. Mama, Daddy, Melanie and I joined other guests as we mounted the broad, curving staircase to the oval ballroom on the second floor. There, the ceiling was at least sixteen feet high with Ionic pilasters and classical moldings accenting the painted walls. A huge mirror reflected the dancers' colorful ball gowns and black tuxedos. A Frazer fir that must have been twelve feet tall filled one long window.

The pipe organ dominated one wall, but Jean Campbell had recently died and there was no one to play it. A small orchestra entertained us with dance tunes, and Mirabelle danced every dance. Crystal chandeliers shone down on her golden head creating a halo-like effect. In a long white tulle dress, she looked like an angel.

Reggie Campbell stood near the entrance, greeting guests, but rarely did his eyes stray from watching Mirabelle. Shelby seemed not to notice. I'd been fascinated, watching him watching her. The look he gave her could only be described as hungry.

Was Melanie right? Were those skeletons Reggie and Shelby? Oh, I hoped not. Let them be someone else, strangers. I visualized the Campbells in Europe, pictured them sailing the Mediterranean, or happily ensconced in a villa in the Tuscan hills. Or sipping thick espresso in a sidewalk cafe in Rome. A tremor ran through my body. Let them be anywhere, but not buried in the wall for six long years.

Mirabelle had a lot of fans. Yet many people felt about her the way Mrs. Burns did, that she was a phony and basically dishonest.

I LOOKED UP and saw Mirabelle walking toward me. "Take this," she said, and thrust her briefcase at me. I caught it before it fell to the floor.

Mirabelle was attractive and I didn't know how old she was, but suspected she was older than she looked. Her complexion was a flawless peachy pink, no wrinkles. Strands of golden blonde hair fell over her forehead in a spiky fringe. Her bright blue eyes scanned the crowd as if she expected to be recognized.

I trotted along beside her as she strode through the atrium as if she owned the airport and everyone who worked in it. She began a running commentary on how dreadful air travel had become, the delays, the beefed-up security. "They made me take off my shoes, for pity sakes!"

I scampered to keep up. Mirabelle was a high-energy person, a workaholic who got by on four hours of sleep, always in a rush, always scheming. A cluster of young women spotted her, pointed excitedly, exclaimed and waved.

Mirabelle stopped, a wide grin causing her to appear approachable, and I realized this is what she'd been waiting for. The lively women surrounded her. As Mirabelle signed autographs, she cast me a helpless look that seemed to ask: What can I do? My public adores me.

"Get my bags for me, will you, sweetie?" she called, pushing claim tickets into my hand. "I'll meet you at your car." She chuckled, as if she thought this fuss over her was absurd. Yet I had gotten to know her well enough to know she maneuvered every situation until she was the center of attention.

Moving toward the baggage claim area, I asked myself, Now how am I going to know which bags are hers? But clever Mirabelle called after me, "Mine are the Louis Vuitton matched pieces with the red bows."

"Why am I not surprised?" I grumbled as a chute opened and luggage spilled onto the revolving carousel. "The Style Maven ties ribbons on her luggage." Two enormous brown vinyl suitcases with the Vuitton stamped emblem and sporting big red bows rode into view.

I hefted the bags off the carousel and looked around for a skycap or at least a luggage cart. Neither. I was on my own. Shoving the briefcase up under my arm, and grabbing the suitcases by their handles, I lugged them through the automatic doors and headed for short-term parking. It couldn't be avoided, I was forced to drag Mirabelle's bags across the hot parking lot. The bottoms of the expensive luggage scraped over the rough pavement then bogged down in pools of tacky asphalt. Why doesn't she buy rugged nylon suitcases with wheels like all us little people? I fumed.

Popping the tailgate of my station wagon, I heaved the expensive luggage inside, almost falling in on top of them. The air smelled of hot tar. I slid in behind the steering wheel and started the motor and air conditioner. Then realized with a frisson of delight that Mirabelle didn't know where I was parked. Serves her right if she burns up out there, I mused, and smiled at the image of Mirabelle wandering up and down rows of parked cars, her ivory silk pantsuit stained with sweat, her makeup melting, her hair flat.

"Let me in!" She tapped on the window. Some fantasies don't come true.

"Oh, sweetie, I don't deserve my good fortune," she cooed as I paid the parking attendant. It would never occur to Mirabelle to fork over a few bucks.

She went on, "Fate has been so good to me. I'd love to tell you my fabulous news but I'm sworn to secrecy."

I cut my eyes her way while checking traffic in both directions. Mirabelle took that brief glance as encouragement. "*Lifetime* Television is syndicating my show," she blurted.

"*Lifetime?*" I asked.

"Yes, *Lifetime*. There. Now you know my secret.

How you do drag things out of me, Ashley Wilkes. You're just like Melanie."

Me? Just like Melanie?

"But you mustn't tell a soul," she went on, "not even her. I don't want those fools out at the production studio to know." She reached over to pat my hand on the steering wheel. "We're such good friends, I know I can count on you."

I merged into peak rush-hour traffic, and headed east. *Lifetime* Television *was* big. So Mirabelle's show *Southern Style* was going to be nationally syndicated. Then the implication of that prospect hit me: how was this news going to affect the restoration of the mansion?

Drawing a deep breath, I began, "Something happened today at the site …"

"The site?" Mirabelle said irritably. "You mean my house, don't you?"

"The house then. *Your* house. Anyway, as I was saying, you should know that …"

But Mirabelle had her own agenda. "You're going to have to move up the schedule, Ashley, sweetie. *Lifetime* is inaugurating their holiday programming with my show. Imagine, li'l ole me, cooking Christmas dinner in my new studio kitchen on live TV with the whole nation watching. I'm so thrilled I can scarcely draw a breath. So, sweetie, you'll just have to tell those carpenter friends of yours to get off their duffs and get a move on. I've got to be in that kitchen and ready to broadcast by December 15th."

"December!" My foot hit the brake abruptly.

"Watch what you're doing, you idiot!" Mirabelle screeched.

"But, Mirabelle, that's only six weeks away."

"Well, who doesn't know that? Is there a problem, sweetie? Because if there is, you'll just have to work it out. You know what I always say: There *are* no problems, only solutions."

I swallowed hard. How could Mirabelle move up the schedule? We had a contract. How did she expect me, with all the structural changes that had to be made, to complete the demolition work and get a new kitchen installed so quickly? I pulled off the crowded highway and drove into a bank's parking lot.

"Now what are you doing? You know I'm in a hurry. You're always so theatrical, Ashley. Just like Melanie. Drama queens, the two of you."

That was news. I took a deep breath, leaned my elbows on the steering wheel, and stared straight ahead. I didn't dare look Mirabelle in the eye. "Uh, Mirabelle, you haven't heard the news, have you? We had a little accident in the house this morning and, well, something really bad has…"

Mirabelle's tone was dangerously calm. She crossed her arms on her chest, and tilted her head to one side like a bird eyeing a worm. "Are you telling me the work has stopped?"

"If you'll just let me explain what happened, I'm sure you'll understand."

Mirabelle pursed her lips. *Now she looks her age,* I thought, all that makeup caked in those little lines. Those weren't laugh lines, either.

"I was warned about you," she declared in a chilly voice. "Every designer in this town, including the esteemed Sheldon Mackie, was salivating to do my house, but as a special favor to Melanie I gave the commission to you—a nobody. Now I'm not going to let some little nobody decorator spoil my big chance with *Lifetime*…"

"I…"

"…because I'll sue your bony ass from here to kingdom come if you don't bring this job in on time!"

"Will you just let me explain!" I banged the steering wheel with my fist; the horn blared. We both jumped.

"All right, I'm listening." Mirabelle fixed me with a hostile glare.

I explained that we'd discovered the skeletons of a man and a woman in the kitchen wall, that the house was a homicide scene, sealed by the police.

Mirabelle stroked her upper arms, then rested her head against the headrest, and let out a whistle. A smile played on her lips. "This is good. Having people say the house was haunted was what attracted me to it in the first place, all that stuff about the ghost organist. I could have bought any number of historic mansions. But this, well you can't buy publicity like this. My ratings will skyrocket. Everyone will tune in to my show just to see a murder site. Ashley, sweetie, you couldn't have given me better news!"

FIVE

"I DON'T KNOW WHY I bother with the entrée list," I told Jon. "I should skip right ahead to the dessert menu. That's what I like best."

"Order whatever you want," he said, giving me "that look" and smiling like his face would break in two.

He's been looking at me in this special way ever since we met. Well, I should correct that: met for the second time. We had met before, years ago, when I was about fourteen, and he about twenty-two and just finishing his undergraduate degree at NC State. Jon Campbell was part of Melanie's crowd. I was the kid sister he never even noticed. Until now.

"Oh, that Mirabelle Morgan. What a piece of work," I said.

After I had driven her home to Landfall, I'd called Jon to fill him in on her latest demands. I knew he'd commiserate with me. She had been making both our lives miserable for weeks. He'd suggested dinner at Port Land Grille at Lumina Station. The days were growing shorter and Lumina sparkled in the darkness like its inspiration, the original Lumina Dance Pavilion, used to light up Wrightsville Beach in the days before the Second World War. Soft breezes from the coast rocked empty white rocking chairs out on the porches.

Inside the restaurant, the lights were soft and the service impeccable. As we shared a bottle of California red, I wondered why life couldn't always be this simple.

Jon refilled my glass. "Don't let Mirabelle get you down." His reputation in the restoration field was outstanding. I was thrilled to be working with him.

I swallowed a large sip of wine. "How does she manage it? This is a woman who does silly things like roll up linen place mats between sheets of tissue paper and ties them with perfect bows. She insisted I get involved with the police investigation. 'Help speed things along,' she said."

Jon's warm brown eyes crinkled merrily. "Shall I start calling you Nancy Drew?"

Our waiter arrived. "Actually, I'm not very hungry. Madam spoiled my appetite. Think I'll just have an appetizer." And I ordered a slice of beef tenderloin with cheese, olives, onion, and crackers. "That should do me fine. What are you having?"

"I need something more substantial. I never did get lunch." To the waiter he said, "I'll have the grilled grouper."

"Good choice," the waiter said, "fresh off the boat this morning at Southport."

After he left, I told Jon, "I know you're trying to make me feel better. I'm ashamed to confess that I did call Detective Yost and left a message for him. I don't want to lose this job. It's my big chance. I'll do anything."

I didn't tell Jon how my heart had beat faster when

I asked for Detective Yost, how I was almost relieved when he wasn't at the station to take my call because I didn't think I could speak to him without gushing.

Jon's hand covered mine on the table. "What can I do to help, Ashley?" I shook my head in frustration. "Just back me up."

"You know I'll do that."

His kindness undid me and my sob-story came pouring out. "Sure I have a contract that gives me until January to complete the kitchen, but what good does that do me? I'm the new girl in town. I've got to prove myself. I don't have the money to get into a protracted legal battle with Mirabelle. And even if I did and won, she would bad-mouth me all over town. She'd destroy me. She's far more powerful than I am."

"Well, the new deadline applies to me too," Jon said. "And Willie."

"Oh, Willie. He's got clients standing in line. And you don't need her, Jon. You're established. Everyone says you're the best. But me, I'm just starting out. She moved the deadline up by a month, then said she'd sue me if I didn't meet it. How did she put it? Sue my bony ass? If only her little groupies could hear her trashy mouth! Yet, to see her on TV, you'd think she was the most proper Southern lady."

Angrily, I attacked the bread basket, pulling an innocent dinner roll apart.

MIRABELLE HAD HAD the nerve to shake hands, as if that meant anything to someone as unscrupulous as our celebrity kitchen maven. Then I drove her home to Landfall, the posh, gated community that had been developed on the former Pembroke Jones hunting preserve.

Mirabelle's maid Sissy had come out to collect the luggage. "There might be some scratches," I told her. "If Mirabelle tries to blame you, let me know. I'll straighten her out." But I certainly wasn't going to pay for designer luggage. Sissy rolled her eyes, like she'd seen it all and nothing "white folks" did could surprise her.

Leaving Landfall, I'd felt sorry for myself, couldn't bear the thought of another evening alone and called Jon. And bless him, he'd suggested Port Land Grille and I'd offered to pick him up. Save the gas and the environment.

Then I'd driven east to the drawbridge that connected the mainland to Wrightsville Beach. Jon lives on the north end of the island in a salmon pink stucco house that backs up to the Intracoastal Waterway.

As luck would have it, the bridge was up. I set my brake, left my car on the ramp, and walked to the guardrail. The sun was setting and the waterway glowed a burnished gold. A familiar brackish scent filled the evening air. I leaned on the rail to watch as a convoy of tall ships passed through the open bridge.

Every Thanksgiving, tall ships sailed out of Banks Channel to parade up and down the waterway. Their masts were decorated with colorful lights in the outlines of Christmas trees and Santa Clauses. Carols float over the water. Wilmingtonians by the hundreds crowded the banks. The Christmas season officially began.

Gazing up at the first star, I'd thought: Does

anyone up there care? Yes! came a resounding reply from the universe.

Pluck up, sweetheart, I heard my daddy whisper.

By Thanksgiving the kitchen would either be well on its way to completion or I'd be a failure. One way or the other, I'd know. *You were created to succeed,* came that sure inner voice.

"REFILL?" JON ASKED, dragging me back to the restaurant and our conversation.

I nodded. "You might have to do the driving."

"You'll be fine," he said. "You'll have coffee and dessert and when we leave, you'll be fine. Now look, I want you to forget about Mirabelle. She's the client from hell and anybody with an ounce of sense knows it. Just concentrate on what this job is going to do for your career when the house is finished. You're talented and this is a great house. It'll lead to many important restorations. You can do it."

"Thanks," I said, tears forming on my lashes. I blinked them away and lifted my chin. "You're right. That house is going to be magnificent again. I'll have more work than I can handle."

Jon took a drink and gave me a long, level look. "Ashley," he began slowly, "would you like to go out sometime?"

I hesitated. "Do you think that's wise? We have to work together every day. Maybe not such a good idea."

His face was so transparent, revealing bitter disappointment.

"How about when the job is finished? We can go out and celebrate," I suggested.

And immediately he brightened. "It's a date!"

Quickly, I changed the subject. "Jon? Exactly how did those bodies get inside that wall? You saw the mess Willie had to make to break through the plaster. And what about noise? You can't knock out a wall without making a racket. Do you think the killer had a sledge-hammer handy, knocked open the wall, removed a section of laths, hid the bodies, nailed the laths back in place, plastered the wall, and repainted?"

Jon lifted a palm. "Whoa! You've forgotten about the dumbwaiter shaft."

I tapped my fingers to my forehead. The dumbwaiter shaft! Of course. The dumbwaiter shaft had been a bone of contention ever since the project began two weeks ago. Mirabelle had wanted to save it. "It'll be fun to show off," she had said. "A novelty. Sheldon Mackie said we should preserve it."

"There's no way we can expand the kitchen to fit all the cooking equipment you require," Jon had argued, "plus a subzero refrigerator, and space for the camera crew and technicians and all their equipment. We've got to break through that shaft. It's an obstacle."

He had turned to me, "Ashley, what do you think?"

"She'll do what I tell her to do," Mirabelle snapped. "Just find a way to work around it."

"Actually, Mirabelle, Jon, it goes against my training to destroy any historical architectural feature …"

Mirabelle looked smug; Jon seemed surprised that I would disagree with him.

"…except a dumbwaiter."

"What?" Mirabelle cried.

"Look, Mirabelle, I know how you feel about these old treasures. I feel the same way. But that shaft is a fire hazard. If you had a fire in the kitchen, that shaft would act like a flue and suck the flames right up to the second floor ballroom before the firemen could get their boots on. I'm sorry, but I'm with Jon. It's got to go."

I made a friend of Jon that day.

Now, I LOOKED at him across the restaurant table and exclaimed, "The dumbwaiter shaft! Of course. The killer got into the wall from the other side, through the dumbwaiter shaft."

"Which is lined with wood panels," Jon reminded me. "He had only to lower the dumbwaiter to the basement, pry off a panel, and hide those bodies inside the wall."

"But why go to all that trouble? Why not just hide the bodies in the shaft?" What a gruesome picture I painted. I'd never sleep tonight. "The house was empty. Even though I saw it for myself, I still can't picture how he got two bodies into that wall. How could they fit in there?"

"I pried off some of the panels for the police," Jon explained. "There was a lot of dead space, some filler materials. A sort of chamber. A perfect tomb. I've seen odder configurations in old-house construction, and I'll bet you have too."

"Yes, come to think of it I have. Do the police have any idea how they were killed?"

"They weren't confiding in me. But they insisted that Willie and I remain to advise the technicians about removing the remaining laths. Didn't want the house to fall in on their heads, they said.

"The technicians packed the bones in boxes, and I overheard someone say that Dr. Banks was driving them to a forensic anthropologist in Durham, some professor at Duke who does consulting work for the State Bureau of Investigation."

Our food arrived and I didn't want to be talking about murder while eating. I'd done that at lunch.

"Exactly how are you related to Reggie and Shelby Campbell?" I asked.

"Oh, very, very distantly," he replied, cutting his grouper with his fork and groaning with pleasure. "I'm starved. I was wondering what I was going to eat when you called." He gave me one of those smiles again. "So glad you did."

I sliced into the beef tenderloin without very much appetite.

"The Reginald Campbell line is from one branch of the Campbell clan, I'm from another. But we're all descended from Duncan Campbell who led 350 settlers from Argyll to the Upper Cape Fear in 1737.

"The Highland Scots were fierce fighters who sided with the Loyalists. They marched to Moore's Creek Bridge but the Patriots were expecting them, removed the bridge's planks and greased the girders."

Jon chuckled. "My ancestors were defeated by greased logs. Some were taken captive, a few escaped and mingled with the citizenry here. My ancestors were on the wrong side of the War of Independence. How's that for irony?"

"So you were never close to Reggie and Shelby?" I asked.

"Oh, we knew each other in high school. Called each other 'Cuz' just to be smart. But Reggie was from money and I wasn't. Makes a difference. Then later his lifestyle was totally different from mine. We had nothing in common."

"What kind of lifestyle?" I asked. "Exotic. Even aberrant."

"Aberrant?"

"They ran with a fast crowd. Orgies. Mate swapping. Kinky sex. Stuff like that." He looked disapproving. "They were bored, Ashley."

"Hmmm," I said thoughtfully. "Melanie told me she bought the house at foreclosure."

"Yeah, I heard about that. If she hadn't snapped it up someone else would have."

"But someone paid the taxes for several years. So if it wasn't the Campbells paying the taxes, then who was it?"

Jon wagged his eyebrows and did a perfect Humphrey Bogart impersonation. "Why, the murderer, sweetheart."

WHEN I LET MYSELF into my bungalow, the telephone was ringing. Detective Yost said irritably, "I've been calling your house for hours, Ms. Wilkes. Are you all right?"

"Yes, I'm fine."

"Do I have to remind you that you discovered two murder victims this morning? There's a murderer on the loose."

"No, you don't have to remind me. I remember."

"Good. OK, you called me. What can I do for you?"

Yost sounded grumpy and tired. This wasn't going as I had planned. Still, I pressed on. "It's more a matter of what I can do for you, Detective. I might be able to help you with the investigation." I held my breath.

"Oh? Do you know something?"

"Well, no. But I thought I could keep my ears open, maybe pick up a clue."

Yost barked out a derisive laugh. "Sorry, I don't mean to be rude. It's just that it's been a rough day. No reason for me to take out my frustration on you."

"No, it isn't," I said firmly. "OK, then you tell me something. How were those people killed?"

The detective took his time answering. "Well, I guess it can't hurt to tell you, it'll be public knowledge soon. Two .38 caliber slugs were found with the bones. So, it looks like they were shot."

"I don't understand. Did the murderer hide the slugs with the bodies? Why not just put them in his pocket to throw away later?"

Yost cleared his throat. "For the slugs to be found with the bones indicates they were lodged inside the bodies at the time of death."

"Oh, sure," I mumbled, feeling like an idiot. What do I know about slugs? "How do you go about identifying old skeletons?"

"We'll x-ray the bones and teeth. Start with the Campbells' dentists and doctors. Compare our X rays with theirs."

"Detective, when can we get back into the house? I'm working on a tight deadline."

"Forensics hasn't finished processing the crime scene yet, but I'll ask them to expedite things, Ms. Wilkes. I'll call you. Soon."

"But with crimes so old, what can you hope to find? Won't the evidence be destroyed by now?"

"Not blood, Ms. Wilkes. Blood traces last forever."

"Oooh. I'd still like to help, Detective. Please call me if I can." "I may do just that," he said smoothly. "Thanks, Ms. Wilkes, I appreciate the offer."

As I got ready for bed and reviewed our conversation, I was sure he had softened.

SIX

EARLY THE NEXT MORNING, I drove to the heart of the historic district. Surveying Orange Street in both directions, I verified that no one from law enforcement was at the house, not the Crime Scene Unit or a patrol car. I strolled casually across the sidewalk, opened the gate, and ducked under yellow crime scene tape. If I ran into a police officer, I planned to tell him I'd spoken to Detective Yost on the phone last night about assisting with the case, which was true. Of course, if I ran into Detective Yost, my posterior was grass, as they say.

Enormous magnolia trees blocked the house from the street. They blocked out the sun too, and the garden lay in deep shade. I stepped onto the portico. Here it was shadowy with scarcely a breath of air. Yellow crime scene tape formed a huge X on the oversized front door.

The keys to this door were missing. Melanie had hired a locksmith to let her inside the first time she looked at the house. The shutters had been closed and secured from the inside, then the windows shut and locked. And the basement windows were covered with plywood.

On a key rack in the butler's pantry, we'd found keys to the back door, a side door, inside doors and cupboards, all neatly labeled. The original locks were huge and ornate, the escutcheons made from solid brass. They were rare, definitely keepers. The key to the front door was never found. Eventually, we'd have a new key made but with a lock so old, that would take time. A temporary lock had been installed. I fingered the smooth warm key in my pocket that fit the new lock.

Clouds rolled in and a cool wind swirled fallen magnolia leaves. Somewhere nearby rain was falling. Darkness settled in under the trees. I walked around the house in the gloom, the dense quiet broken only by the wind rattling the loose shutters. Turning a corner, I came face to face with a large bearded man carrying a grim-reaper scythe. Startled, I jumped back.

"Didn't mean to frighten you, Miss, but you are trespassing," he asserted. Yet his voice was lyrical, distinctly Scots Highlander.

I looked up into a hairy face with pale blue eyes as cold as ice chips. "I am not trespassing," I declared. "I have every right to be here. What are you doing here?"

He pulled off a threadbare cap, evidence that someone had once taught him manners. "I look after the garden. Henry Cameron is my name. And who might you be?"

"Where did you come from?" I asked. "I didn't seen a car or truck parked at the curb."

"I'm parked up yonder, in the alley." He motioned with the sharp-bladed scythe. I flinched.

He frowned at me. "Mite skittish, ain't you, miss?" He propped the savage tool against a tree.

Beyond some overgrown oleander bushes, I spotted

an ancient, dented pickup truck in the alley. Rust held it together like brown glue.

"Miz Campbell asked me to look after her house till she came home."

"You know Mrs. Campbell?"

"You sure ask a lot of questions for a trespasser who ain't got any business being here. You still haven't told me who you are. This place is my responsibility and I don't allow no squatters."

"The house has been sold, Henry," I said trying to let him down gently. He looked like he was poor, and now he was out of a job. "I'm restoring it for the new owner. My name is Ashley Wilkes."

"What! Sold? New owner? Oh, no, miss, that can't be. Miz Campbell would never sell. Why, she loved this place."

"Where is Mrs. Campbell? People have been looking for her for years." Was that true? Was anyone looking for her? Maybe just the tax collector.

"Mr. and Miz Campbell are traveling abroad, Miss. I get letters and cards from them from time to time. Distant lands. Exotic places."

"Recently?"

He stroked his beard thoughtfully. "Well, no, not recently. But from time to time, like I say. She sent me money and told me to keep an eye on things. I had to board up the basement windows because squatters was trying to get inside. Had to padlock some of the doors too. That front door's burglar proof. Too solid. Too heavy."

"Do you have the key to the front door?" I asked. "It's missing."

"Don't have keys to any of the doors, Miss. I wasn't asked to take care of the inside. Just to look after the outside. Make sure no one broke in. And the front door key ain't missing, Mr. and Miz Campbell have it."

"Those were your specific instructions? To not let anyone inside?" I asked, thinking that Henry Cameron had not heard the news.

"Specific enough. Miz Campbell said she didn't want nobody poking around inside *her* house."

"Well, nobody has, Henry. Not for six years. Not until two weeks ago."

I wondered how he could have been so out of touch he hadn't heard about the skeletons I'd found. The radio, television, and newspapers were covering the story.

Perhaps he'd been in the mountains, somewhere so remote they didn't get the news. And that truck, it might not have a radio.

Henry was gazing over my shoulder and frowning. "Now what's all this crime scene tape? What's been going on here? Have they been robbed?"

As I GOT IN MY CAR, I asked myself: If Shelby Campbell had hired Henry Cameron to be a sort of caretaker, who was the woman buried in the wall? Had Shelby Campbell caught her husband in the arms of another woman and in a fit of jealous rage shot them both? No, I rejected that idea. Shelby was very petite. She would not have been capable of moving two bodies and stowing them deep inside the wall. Unless, she had help. An accomplice. And now she and her accomplice were living abroad somewhere, living lavishly on Reggie Campbell's fortune.

SEVEN

I PUSHED OPEN my studio door to find an envelope shoved under it. Legal size and thick. I recognized the return address. Mirabelle's attorneys. Just as I suspected, a handshake meant nothing to the queen of pots and pans. I dropped the envelope on my desk, delaying the inevitable.

When I'd set up my studio in a restored carriage house on Chandler's Wharf, I was certain I'd be flooded with demands for my services. Gentrification in the historic district had taken hold. Celebrities like Linda Lavin were buying up old houses and restoring them. The last of Daddy's legacy had gone for rent, business and personal expenses. Now, there was little money left. I had to placate Mirabelle no matter how abused I felt.

I slit open the envelope and slid the documents out. Mirabelle's lawyers had drawn up a contract reflecting the new deadline. They must have stayed up all night. Oh, Daddy, why aren't you here when I need you? I slammed my fist down on my desk, flinched at the pain, then picked up the contract and read the fine print. If the new kitchen was not ready for use on December 15, I could kiss my commission goodbye. My stomach knotted painfully.

I had to get a grip on my fears. OK, she's the boss, I told myself, for now. Not forever. As soon as this job is complete, I'll never have to see her again. There'll be other clients. Success was as near as the close Southern air. I vowed I'd survive any trap my "Client from Hell" set for me.

The sound of tapping came from the back room. Tommy, an upholsterer who shared space and rent with me, was already at work. He was a part-timer, a retiree from a high-end furniture company in High Point. If bluefish were running, or if tuna were sighted off the coast, Tommy blew me a kiss and vanished for days.

We had an arrangement that worked to our mutual benefit: I sent business his way, he gave my work top priority. As tight as money was for me, I was lucky to have him sharing the expenses on the studio. And it was good to have someone around to talk to. Plus, he was the best in his craft.

I joined him in the back to check on furniture from Campbell House that he was reupholstering. The workroom was spacious, strikingly colorful with bolts of brightly patterned cottons and linens, silk damasks and voiles, all wrapped in clear plastic bags.

Tommy, barrel-chested and brawny-armed from years of manhandling heavy pieces, was pulling upholstery tacks out of an authentic Duncan Phyfe sofa. The framework was carved with the acanthus leaf motif.

"Squirrels sure did a number on this one," he said, referring to shredded damask.

"I know. Somehow animals got into the house."

"Where's the new cloth you want me to use?"

I pointed to a bolt of Schumacher velvet in soft celadon green. "We'll use that for the furniture. I think we can save the Aubusson rug. It's got those same shades of green. Somehow it withstood the damp."

Tommy picked up a small object off the worktable and handed it to me. "Found that way down behind the seat cushion."

A lovely cameo brooch of fine quality rested in my palm. The stone was a pale coral color with dainty seed pearls mounted around the oval. I knew that brooch.

"Thanks," I said. "I'll put this in a safe place."

"That must've been some shock for you, Ashley, finding that skull. It's all the TV reporters are talking about."

"It was pretty grisly."

"Well, if you need anything, anything a' tall, you know you can count on me."

I wrapped an arm around his shoulders. "I know, Tommy. And thanks."

"Everyone's saying those remains are Mr. and Mrs. Campbell," he went on. "I did some work for them years back."

"You knew them?"

"Yep, sure did. Fact is, I'm the one put on this here yeller cover." He eyed the dirty damask that showed patches of delicate yellow. "That was about seven years ago, right after I took early retirement and moved here so I could fish."

"They invited me to their Christmas party when I was seventeen. That was the last time I saw them."

"Never met him but I do remember her right well. Pretty woman. Nice too. Down to earth for a rich woman. None of that highfalutin stuff like I've had to put up with some. She liked to kick back and have herself a bit of fun. I went over there one evening to give her an estimate, and before I knew it she was whipping up whiskey sours and we was having ourselves a high old time."

He paused, his expression softening. "You know, Ashley, she seemed right lonely to me. A sad little thing. But she tried not to let it show. I felt kinda sorry for that little lady."

I remembered Jon's comment about the group sex parties the Campbells used to host. That would sure do me in. I wanted to ask Tommy what time he left Shelby Campbell's house that night or if he left at all. He was still vigorous for a man in his sixties. Seven years ago, he was younger and even more virile. He was a widower then and lonely, and if Shelby was lonely and unhappy, perhaps they had comforted each other.

"And Reggie Campbell didn't come home?" I asked.

"Not that night." He clamped his mouth shut and cast me a furtive glance.

I pretended I hadn't heard the slip. "Maybe he was away on business."

"Humph! What business? Man never worked a day in his life. Like they say, he earned his money the old-fashioned way—inherited it."

Apparently in Tommy's book, an idler was a worse sinner than an adulterer.

"Hate to think of that pretty woman being left inside a wall like that. Not even getting a decent Christian burial."

"Now, Tommy, we don't know yet who those skeletons are. The police are trying to make an identification."

"It's got to be them. Who else could it be? Nobody else is missing, are they?"

Good question, I thought. Detective Yost would know about missing persons. Detective Yost was the key to everything. Now if I could only find some way to ingratiate myself with him.

EIGHT

I HADN'T SEEN Teddy Lambston since high school, so it was a surprise to find him waiting for me in my studio after lunch. "Well, I declare, Teddy, what are you doing here?" *I declare?* How quickly we revert to downhome-isms.

Teddy shot to his feet. "Hey, Ashley!" He held out his arms and I walked into them. We hugged. Teddy had always been such a sweet guy in high school. I remembered that in junior high, he'd taken a lot of ribbing about being a mama's boy. Then in high school there were rumors that he was gay, but I didn't listen to the gossip. Just because he's not macho, I reasoned, doesn't mean he's homosexual. And so what if he is? That's nobody's business but his.

Teddy hadn't changed much since high school. His curly, honey-blonde hair was tied back in a pony tail, the way he'd worn it then.

I remembered how he used to call me up and we'd gossip on the phone for hours. Then I went away to college and we lost touch. Even when I came home for holidays, I never ran into Teddy.

"I came by to say hey because we're going to be working together. Isn't that great? It'll be like old times."

Confused, I said, "That's terrific, Teddy, but what do you mean?"

"I'm Mirabelle's new assistant."

For a moment I was speechless. "Well, congratulations. That's wonderful. You know, we really have some catching up to do. I haven't seen any of the old crowd in ages. So you're working for Mirabelle now? How well do you know her?"

"We've only just met, but already I like her. She has a way of making you feel special, don't you think?"

Oh, dear, this was bad. Poor Teddy, he was always such an innocent and so gullible. I suppressed a giggle. Little "Lambston" being led to the slaughter. "Oh, very special. What will you be doing for Mirabelle?"

"Well, for right now, I'll be the liaison regarding the kitchen remodeling. I'll help expedite things."

Liaison? That's all we needed on this project, one more person to slow things down. Then I reconsidered. Maybe Teddy could help, act as a buffer between me and Mirabelle when she got into one of her huffy moods. He was such a pussycat, perhaps he could placate her. Yeah, dream on, Wilkes. No one could.

So busy was I plotting my strategy, I almost missed what he said next. "My degree is in television production, you know, and I've had good experience, so once the *Lifetime* series begins, I'll be assisting the producer. Till then, you can call me with questions about the kitchen and I'll get back to you with Mirabelle's answers."

He seemed to sense his new role might be an intrusion. "Sorry, Ashley, it's the way she wants it."

"That's OK, Teddy. Not your fault. And, you know, this might be for the best. Sit down. Let's catch up. Where have you been all these years?"

Teddy surveyed my studio, admiring the colorful tools of my trade. "I like what you've done here, Ashley."

Bookcases were filled with catalogues offering vintage fixtures. Reproduction wallpaper books were stacked on the shelves, and sample cards of fabric swatches hung from pegs. An antique Welsh cupboard had been put to use as a display case for gimp and fringes, long silky tassels, brass hardware. Teddy was impressed, yet had no way of knowing I wasn't going to be able to pay the rent here much longer.

"Sometimes I think I should have gone into decorating," he mused out loud. "I have a flair for it like mother did."

"Yes, I remember how talented she was. And you were one of the best artists in school."

"But instead I studied television production at New York University."

"New York University! I don't believe this! I went to Parsons. It's on Fifth Avenue and Thirteenth Street. We were just blocks apart."

"Both of us in New York at the same time! Oh, and wasn't 9/11 awful? They closed the school for a while."

"Mine too," I said.

"My mother wanted me to come home, but like I told her: Lightning doesn't strike twice. It seemed disloyal to leave after that."

"I know just what you mean."

We were silent for a while, remembering the tragedy and the sadness that followed.

"No one in the old gang seemed to know where you were," I said. "I asked about you every time I came home. It would have been fun to get together in New York. Someone from home to share that horrible event with. But you're here now. Maybe we can go out some night."

"There are some new clubs," Teddy responded. "We can try them out. I've got some catching up to do. I didn't come home much, spent my school breaks in New York, so much to do there. Of course, I came back when mother died."

"I heard about that, Teddy. I'm so sorry."

"Thanks, Ashley. Anyway, two years ago, I moved back to North Carolina to work at UNC-TV in Chapel Hill. I've been trying to find a job in television back here in Wilmington for a year, but that's not easy. I lucked out when Mirabelle offered me a spot on her show."

I could understand why he felt grateful to Mirabelle. Wasn't I in the same boat?

"How awful for you, Ashley, to find those skeletons. Do the police have any idea who they are and how they got in Shelby and Reggie's house?"

"I don't know what the police think, Teddy, but everyone I talk to says they must be Shelby and Reggie."

Teddy gasped. "Oh, don't say that! It's like you're putting a curse on them. They're very much alive. Mother used to get cards and letters from them from all over Europe. Did you know they partied with the royals? Fergie and her crowd."

He got a dreamy look on his face. "I remember one summer they rented a villa in Tuscany. It had a romantic name, something like Santa Angela, or some name that had 'angel' in it. They invited me to visit but I was in summer school that year."

"Are you sure, Teddy? Because this is critical information. You need to tell the police. Do you think your mother saved the postcards?"

"Well, I don't know if she saved them or not but I'm sure about her receiving them. Most of our neighbors on Orange Street got postcards from all over Europe. Ask Sherman and Muffie Warner. Their house is right next door to Reggie and Shelby's, and they were best friends. I know they got them too."

Teddy seemed so sure of what he was saying, I didn't know what to believe.

"Well, I've got to go, Ashley. It's been great seeing you. Stop by my house some day. I'd like to show you what I'm doing to it. Mother left it to me, free and clear."

"Sure. I'd like to. Is our meeting with Mirabelle still on for tomorrow morning?"

"Yes. She said to remind you to be on time." He spread his hands apologetically. "She's a stickler for detail. That's the secret of her success. She's a very hands-on business woman."

After he left, I shook my head. Poor Teddy, what have you gotten yourself into?

As I stared out the window at Chandler's Wharf, a truly incredible thought occurred to me. If Reggie and Shelby

NINE

THE HOUSE I grew up in is one of the prettiest houses in Wilmington on one of the prettiest streets, Summer Rest Road. With three tiers of lacy white verandas across the front, and a widow's walk on top, it resembles a three-layer wedding cake. The porches and long windows offer spectacular views of the Intracoastal Waterway.

I parked on a slip of brick pavers in front of the cottage next door where I lived now, a small blue bungalow with pretty shrubs and a white picket fence. Melanie's SUV was not parked in Mama's driveway. I got out of my car and gave the marshes, sandbars, and distant Wrightsville Island a long, loving look. At the end of our pier, Melanie's sleek red speedboat bobbed in the water.

Melanie must have come by boat and docked at Mama's. The weather was perfect for cruising the waterway. Perhaps she and her new mystery beau had taken the boat out for a spin earlier. I wondered again who he was and if he was anyone I knew.

Someone was sitting in the boat and for one heart-stopping second I thought it was Daddy. But Daddy passed on six years ago, during my first year at Parsons. When I was a teenager, and we three bickering women got on his nerves, he'd escape to his fishing boat. He'd sit out there at the end of the pier, tying flies or just idling time, waiting for the storm to pass in our house.

I lifted a hand to shade my eyes from the bright noonday sun. The stowaway was my mother, wearing one of Daddy's old fishing hats. It was so dangerous for her to be out on the water. I hurried to the end of the pier, quietly, not wanting to startle her.

"Mama, you OK?"

She lifted her eyes and regarded me suspiciously. These days she almost always looked confused and fearful. "Go away! This is my private pier." Agitated, she stood up and darted from one end to the other, rocking the boat perilously.

I reached my arms out to steady her but she only backed toward the bow. "Don't make any sudden movements, Mama," I said, gingerly stepping down into the small craft. If I wasn't careful, we'd both fall overboard.

I hated seeing her this way—agitated, scared. Wisps of gray hair poked out from under the soft, faded hat. Her hair was too long, but she wouldn't let anyone cut it, not even when Melanie begged. It used to be the prettiest shade of auburn.

She backed further away from me. The rocking turned violent.

"Stand still, Mama. Don't move!"

"Why are you calling me Mama? I'm nobody's mama."

At least she stopped moving. You're my mama, I thought, and I've always needed more of you than you were willing to give. Now, it's too late. How can you love me when you don't even know me?

I stretched out my hands and grasped hers, speaking gently as if to a child. "It's me, Claire. Ashley. Take my hand. Come with me. We don't want to overturn the boat. You'll get wet and the water's cold."

"Ashley who?" she asked. Her once erect figure of which she'd been so proud was now stooped. She cast about erratically, searching for some other way out. I was afraid she'd jump. The boat wobbled.

"I'm Ashley Wilkes. Your daughter."

She seemed to brighten. "Oh, Ashley Wilkes. What a fine young gentleman. No wonder Scarlett loved him. What woman wouldn't? If I ever have a son, I'll name him Ashley Wilkes."

"You have two daughters, Claire. And you named me Ashley, and my sister Melanie."

Mama seemed not to hear. "Such a fine gentleman," she went on, speaking of Margaret Mitchell's Ashley.

Melanie and I could never understand our mother's fascination with *Gone With the Wind*. At times, the fictional characters seemed more real to her than her own family.

I wanted her back in the real world with me. I wished there was something I could do to make things better for her, restore things to the way they used to be. I wanted her to stroke my hair and tell me she was proud of me, that she loved me as much as I loved her.

The morning clouds had lifted and sun shone on the golden marshes where pelicans and egrets nested. It was so peaceful here. How I'd loved growing up on the waterway, exploring, discovering nature. There was nothing like this view, the smell of the marshes, the glimpses of colorful cottages on Wrightsville Beach. Already the nights were cooler. Autumn, my favorite time of year.

"Come on, Mama," I said, taking her hand and helping her out of the boat. "Nellie's fixing lunch for us and I brought you a new CD."

Mama didn't eat much these days; she'd become quite thin. I didn't know how much longer we'd be able to keep her at home. Yet, I worried that leaving the home she loved might make her deeply depressed.

Safely on the boardwalk, she pulled her arm out of my grasp and gave me an odd look. "I know who killed them."

"Killed who?" A frisson of fear niggled my spine.

"Them. You know. The skeletons."

So even Mama had seen those news broadcasts.

She winked at me. "Scarlett did it."

I took her arm. "Come on, Mama. I brought you the new Enya CD. We'll listen to it together while Nellie sets the table. You know how much you like Celtic music."

She was calmer now and allowed me to walk her to the house. We sat together on the sofa in her living room and allowed Enya's angelic singing to calm both our fears.

NELLIE HAD PREPARED all of Mama's favorite dishes: corn bread and pinto beans, sliced fresh tomatoes and cucumbers that were still being harvested locally. I love the last, tart tomatoes of the season. For dessert there was strawberry short cake with real whipped cream. And, of course, sweet iced tea.

Mama pushed her food around on her plate and ate very little. Melanie watched her with an impatient gleam in her eyes.

"Ummm," Mama said, pointing to the sugar bowl. The old Mama would have said, "Pass the sugar, please, Melanie." The old Mama had been a stickler for proper table manners and had instilled ladylike behavior in her girls.

Mama ladled extra sugar into her tea. I lost count after five teaspoons. I pretended not to see, but Melanie never pretended. She had shouldered the burden of caring for Mama while I'd been away at school. I had no right to criticize. Melanie had done the best she could.

It didn't seem to bother her when she had to correct our mother, as if Mama were the child and Melanie the mother.

"That's enough, Mama," she said firmly, taking the spoon from her hand.

Mama peeked at Melanie through strands of unruly hair. She lifted the iced tea defiantly and drank it down quickly, all the while fixing Melanie with a guarded stare, as if she expected Melanie to take the glass out of her hand too.

"Be nice to her," I whispered. "Mama, do you want another glass of tea?" I lifted the pitcher but she didn't respond.

Nellie was a blessing. When I arrived home in the summer, Melanie had sat me down for a serious talk. "Thank goodness, you're finally home because I can't do this by myself any longer. I've gone through four housekeepers in the past year. None of them last. They all say the same thing: she needs a nursing home. And she does. Dr. Wilmot says it's time to consider a memory care facility."

"No!" I exclaimed.

"Ashley, get real. She's a danger to herself. I'm afraid she's going to fall off the pier. She's always sneaking down there, says she's going fishing with Daddy. I'm so thrilled with Nellie, she's been a godsend. Don't you ever do anything to make her unhappy."

"I won't," I promised. "And I'll spend more time with Mama."

To my amazement right after lunch, Mama became quite her old self. I'd seen this happen before, as if the cobwebs in her brain had been swept away so that she became clear and lucid. "Come up to my room with me, girls," she said with a take-charge tone. "We have urgent business to attend to."

Melanie and I exchanged puzzled glances. It was seldom we heard Mama speak with her former authority.

Mama opened drawers and pulled out jewelry cases. Springing lids, she removed bracelets and necklaces and arranged them on the bedspread where they glittered in shafts of sunlight from the windows. Perched on the edge of the old rosewood bed that had belonged to Grandmere and Grandpere Chastain, she fondled the jewels. Settling beside her, I slipped my arm around her tiny waist. She felt like a bird. Now that she knew me, I hoped she'd say something memorable, something I could hold in my heart to retrieve on the bad days.

"I've decided to give you girls my jewelry while I'm still alive," she said. "No need to wait for me to die."

"Mama! Don't say that."

"Hush now, Ashley. We're going to divide it fairly, and I want you girls to take it home with you today. I don't want to hear any arguments. I know what's happening to me. But I'm having a good spell now, and I promised myself I'd do this the next time my mind cleared."

She knew what was happening to her and was facing it. Tears flooded my eyes.

"Wipe away those foolish tears, Ashley Wilkes. Here, move a little closer and we'll go through this jewelry, piece by piece. You too, Melanie."

This was how she used to be. Maybe her hair was wild and her clothes in disarray, but as she identified family heirlooms she'd inherited, she was our mother again.

"Ruby got the house," she said, "and I got the jewels. Now, Melanie, I want you to have my mama's pearls. They suit you. They're creamy like your skin. Mind you wear them often. The warmth and oils from your skin imparts their patina. There are many grades of pearls, but these are the finest."

Leading Melanie to the dressing table, Mama drew back her hair and fastened a double strand of matched pearls around her long, slender neck. She stood back to admire Melanie in the mirror. My sister was so beautiful. Mama clipped pearl earrings to Melanie's earlobes. My parents' wedding picture sat atop a bureau. In those days Mama was as beautiful as Melanie is now.

"Ashley, for you I thought Great-Aunt Lily's rubies.

They go with your white skin and dark hair. You are so much like your daddy with your sweet little heart-shaped face and eyes so dark gray and serious. Such a handsome man he was. Oh, if only you could have seen him when we first met." She clapped her hands together and giggled like a schoolgirl.

The cool rubies and platinum felt heavy on my neck and I was riddled with guilt. "Mama, you don't have to do this now. There's plenty of time."

"Yes, Ashley, I do. I trust that you girls will do the right thing for me. I can't make decisions for myself, but I'd like to stay here in my home for as long as I can."

"Oh, Mama, I'll move in here and help take care of you," I cried.

She smiled sweetly. "No, Ashley dear. You're a grown woman now and need to live your own life."

I couldn't stand this discussion another minute. I jumped up and ran for the door. Tears flooded my eyes. I turned back to see a blurry Melanie pawing through the jewels on the bed. She knew Mama loved her. She didn't have to watch for signs of it.

"Mama?" she cried. "Where's Aunt Lily's brooch? You know, that sweet little coral-colored cameo with the seed pearls around it?"

"Why, honey, I haven't seen that thing in years. I gave it to you."

TEN

ROY'S RIVERBOAT LANDING Restaurant has private balconies on the second floor, accessed through French doors, and furnished with a cozy table for two. From our lofty height Jon and I overlooked Riverwalk, Riverfront Park, and the water beyond.

I tapped a blue line on the blueprints he'd unrolled. "That's the wall where we found the skeletons."

"As soon as we can get back inside, we'll finish tearing down the walls around the dumbwaiter shaft, then bridge it with a floor and ceiling. Let me show you the new drawings I've made for our meeting with Mirabelle tomorrow."

I studied the details. "They're perfect, Jon, just what we discussed. But you know Mirabelle, she'll find something to criticize." I shook my head. "I wish we'd left that dumbwaiter shaft alone, just sealed up the doors."

"Couldn't. It was in the way. You said yourself it was a fire hazard. And if we'd left it, those bodies would have been hidden in there forever."

I sighed. "If only they had been! We'd be on schedule now, instead of locked out of the house while the police take their own sweet…"

Shrill toots drowned out my words. The stern-wheeler

Henrietta III was paddling away from Riverboat Landing, setting sail for a dinner-dance cruise on the Cape Fear River. Music from the decks floated to our balcony, and laughing voices carried on river breezes.

"I've never done that," I said wistfully.

"Tell you what, as soon as this kitchen is finished, we'll celebrate with a cruise. Would you like that?"

"I'd love it." Our eyes locked and we smiled. We were building a close friendship; I trusted Jon. "To our cruise." We clinked glasses.

The waiter arrived with our plates. Jon rolled a rubber band around the blueprints and thrust them under his chair.

"Men get to enjoy all the rich food. If I ate like you do I'd weigh three hundred pounds."

"Have you ever had this? Here, take a taste." He dipped his fork into "Crowned Seafood Wilmington" and offered it to me. Shrimp and scallops on a crabmeat pate, with cream sauce and puff pastry points.

"Yum, scrumptious." I sampled my chippano, a seafood bouillabaisse made of tuna, salmon, clams, and shrimp over linguine in a delicate clam sauce. "This is heavenly."

As we ate, I filled Jon in on my conversation with Teddy Lambston. "Teddy said his mother got postcards from Reggie and Shelby from all over Europe. So did most of their neighbors on Orange Street: Sherman and Muffie Warner, in particular. Teddy says the Warners were Reggie and Shelby's best friends."

Jon broke off a chunk of dinner roll and popped it in his mouth. "The police will question them."

"Tommy says Shelby seemed unhappy."

"Tommy Comer? Your Tommy? He knew Shelby?"

"Yes. He went over there one evening to give her an estimate on reupholstering some furniture, and Jon…." I giggled "…I think he spent the night with her." The one-night stand between Tommy and Shelby made me uncomfortable. "Tommy let it slip. Then he seemed embarrassed that he had, so I pretended I hadn't heard. He said she was sad."

Jon frowned. "Shelby came on to me once too. She didn't seem offended when I turned her down. It was like she didn't really care, like she was going through the motions."

"Tommy said she was a good sport. That she was nice but unhappy. He really liked her."

"Oh, she was very likeable. So was Reggie. But their style was too loose for me."

"What do you mean?"

"This is what happened. They invited me to one of their parties. After dinner, Shelby explained the game to me. The women would retire to the guest bedrooms upstairs. Each woman was to hang an article of clothing on the doorknob, something she'd been seen wearing earlier. The men were supposed to make their selections and join the women inside. It was an old country-house entertainment they'd picked up in England. You know how decadent the Anglos are, and their boring country weekends. Shelby laughed and said that next time they were going to have the men hang their neckties on the door knobs."

"Oh, Jon, how tacky." I wrinkled my nose.

"I felt the same way. When I got a whiff of what was going on, I thanked her for dinner and I was out of there. I never accepted another invitation."

"I wonder if their little games backfired. Maybe someone got hurt. By the way, who were the members of this group of swingers?"

"Let's see, there were the Cushmans, Gordon and Cecily. You remember her. She's the big true-crime writer. She's made so much money with her books, they've got a house on Orange Street and a beach house.

"And as you said, Sherman and Muffie Warner who live next door to Reggie and Shelby. Sara Beth Franks, the artist. I suppose now they're all suspects."

"Yes, but suspects in whose murder? Till the skeletons are identified, we don't know who died."

"My money's on Reggie and Shelby."

"Guess mine is too." I decided to take Jon into my confidence. "Jon, I think Melanie might have been friends with Shelby and Reggie too."

"Melanie? I never saw her with them. We were all in high school together, but after school, we all went away to college and drifted apart. Why do you think Melanie was involved with them?"

"Tommy found an antique brooch that had slipped down inside Shelby's sofa. That brooch is Melanie's. So she was in their house sometime before they were murdered. Or before they moved away. Or whatever became of them."

"Maybe she lost it when she was looking at the house to buy it," Jon suggested.

"She'd never have sat on that sofa then. It was filthy. No, she lost that brooch when Shelby and Reggie lived there. She was with them."

Out of the corner of my eye I glimpsed a figure standing just inside the open French doors. I turned to him, thinking he was our waiter and I'd been craving Roy's famous chocolate rum cake. Instead of the waiter, I caught Detective Yost staring at me, the kind of look a man gives a woman when no one's watching. Naked. Raw. Embarrassment flickered across his face for an instant, then disappeared. How long had he been standing there? And how much had he heard?

Jon leaned forward and they shook hands. While the two men sized each other up, I regained my composure.

"Good evening, Miss Wilkes."

"Good evening, Detective Yost." Now it was my turn to study him, but I did so openly.

Again, he was dressed beautifully in a summer-weight, light charcoal pinstripe suit over a blue shirt with a red-and-blue rep tie. He held a drink that looked like scotch.

I glanced down to check my own outfit and reassured myself I was appropriately dressed in black silk slacks and a white silk shirt. "You must be off duty, Detective."

"Off duty but never off the job, Miss Wilkes," he replied with a cocky grin.

I smiled. "Glad to see you have a sense of humor."

He smiled back. "I was going to call you later but when I saw you and Mr. Campbell out here, I decided to give you folks the good news. Forensics is finished with the house. You can go back inside whenever you want."

"That is good news. I'd invite you to join us out here but there's scarcely enough room for our two chairs."

"I'm fine where I am," he said and leaned a shoulder against the doorjamb.

Nick Yost was a very self-contained man. Or was that part of the facade? Again I wondered how much he had heard.

I looked from Yost to Jon. Two really attractive men had come into my life. But the charge I felt, like a current of high-voltage electricity, flowed from Nick Yost. He was one sexy guy.

ELEVEN

I LOVED COMING HOME to my cozy cottage on Summer Rest Road. Before Mama got ill, she'd promised me I could live in the small blue cottage she owned next door when I returned home after college.

I'd spent most of the money I'd inherited from Daddy on school and on start-up costs for my business. Now I was living on the last of it. I'd had practically nothing to spend on furnishings for my first home, but paint is cheap.

It took a week to paint the bungalow's four rooms. Selecting pastel hues that replicated the colors of the seascape outside my windows—the pale blues of the waterway and the sky, the golden pallet of the sun-washed marshes—I transformed the inside of my house into a place of warmth and hominess.

A trip in a U-Haul truck to Mama's ancestral home in Savannah yielded treasures fit for a fine antiques shop. From the treasure trove in the attic, Aunt Ruby had generously donated love seats and armchairs, chests of drawers and bibelots. She had been so dear, enthusiastically helping me to furnish my little home. My favorite find was a rice bed, its head and foot boards and four posters in mint condition.

A wide, combination living-dining room dominated

the front of my house. I'd chosen cool blue for its walls, icy white trim, and sisal for the hardwood floor. That was when I'd first connected with Tommy, and I'd had him upholster two mismatched love seats in heavy white cotton twill.

I kicked off my sandals, undressed and took a long warm shower, then slipped into thin cotton pajamas.

I was padding over to my bedtable to check my phone messages when a frantic knocking on my door drew me out into the living room. Surely, that's not Mama, I thought. It was much too dangerous for her to be wandering around outside at night.

Peeping through the sidelight, I saw Nellie, Mama's live-in companion. "Just a sec," I called, dashing into the bedroom to pull on a light cotton robe.

I opened the door quickly. "Is something wrong with Mama, Nellie?"

Nellie is plump with a shiny face, naturally optimistic and cheerful. But tonight she was agitated, twisting her hands. "It's not an emergency, Ashley, but we need to talk."

"Sure, come on in. Can I get you something to drink?" I guided the overwrought woman to the love seat under the window. The moment I'd been dreading had arrived.

When Nellie replied that she didn't care for anything, I sat down next to her and patted her arm. "Now what's wrong? Something's got you upset, Nellie."

"Yes, I am upset," she said firmly, her hands squeezed together in her lap. "You and your sister have got to make other arrangements for your mother. She's past the point where I can take care of her. She's a threat to her own safety!"

"Tell me what happened?"

"I got her ready for bed, then went down to the kitchen to wash up the supper dishes. When I finished, I saw that the front door was standing open. I found your mother down at the end of the pier in her nightgown. She was teetering on the end of it and I thought she'd fall in and drown before I could reach her."

"Oh, Nellie, I am so sorry." I was sorry for Nellie and sorry for Mama and sorry for me. "I'll call Melanie. I promise we'll do something. Please, stay with us until we can make arrangements to get her into a care facility."

She seemed relieved. "I will, Ashley. I won't leave you high and dry. You can count on me."

As we said goodnight, I gave her a hug. "Thank you, Nellie." I wanted to tell her how good she was but thought that might seem condescending.

I dialed Melanie's numbers repeatedly before I went to bed. Each time I got voice mail. "Call me right away. I don't care how late it is," I said. "It's about Mama."

Melanie and Mama had always been close, but during my first year at Parsons something changed. There was a coolness between them that I didn't understand. About that time Mama got sick. Probably she'd been showing signs earlier, but we'd just chalked it up to forgetfulness and her own vague personality. Now we had a major decision to make. I wanted Mama to be safe.

I'd stopped at Melanie's house on my way home from dinner with Jon. I wanted to catch her expression when I handed her the brooch. I'd know just by looking at her if something was amiss. Then I'd get her to explain how the brooch got in Shelby Campbell's sofa. But Melanie hadn't been at home, so my sleuthing would have to wait.

My thoughts turned inward to six years ago when I'd done the unthinkable and left my small-town Southern home to go to school in the big city of New York. The first Christmas I came home, the atmosphere had been tense and strained. At twenty-six Melanie had moved back home so that she could save money to buy her own house. Melanie and Mama treated each other politely but coolly. They didn't quarrel, but there was some undercurrent, something was really wrong between them.

On Christmas eve, Daddy drank more than I'd ever seen him do, fortifying the eggnog with Southern Comfort. In the evening, he went out, saying he had to retrieve some papers he'd forgotten at the court house. He never returned. He'd driven into one of the enormous Live Oak trees on Airlie Drive. He died in the ambulance on the way to the hospital. That was the worst Christmas, the worst day, of my life.

I slipped off my robe and curled up on the bed, waiting for Melanie's call. I must have dozed off for the sudden chirp of my bedside phone woke me with a start. Melanie said irritably, "Whatever's wrong, Ashley, you'll have to handle it. I'm not alone."

TWELVE

THE NEXT MORNING, in preparation for our meeting with Mirabelle, I dressed in a black skirt and red sweater set. Red for power, red for energy, red for danger. Red that warned: Don't mess with me!

I met Jon at the big doors to Down East Productions where Mirabelle's show *Southern Style* was being telecast live. He looked professional in a navy blazer and gray slacks. One of the things I like about my hometown is that men still wear suits and sports jackets.

Over the door, a red light glowed, signaling that filming was in progress. Jon and I tiptoed inside, were motioned to the sidelines and signaled to be quiet. As I watched the show unfold, I observed another of Mirabelle's many faces. The woman was a chameleon. Today her role was all-knowing Earth Mother, patiently instructing her untutored children in the fine art of Christmas wreath construction.

The set was done up like a homey country kitchen with bouquets of dried herbs hanging overhead, an arrangement of vegetables in an enamel bowl on a large scrubbed-pine table. Mirabelle was dressed in a blue denim work shirt, its tail hanging out over khaki pants. With nails unvarnished and fingers unadorned, her capable hands flew through the tasks of a hard-working country woman. Flyaway bangs fell in her eyes and she was constantly brushing them aside with a flip of the wrist.

Two immense television cameras zoomed in on the craft project. A cameraman hunched into his camera, a turned-around baseball cap covering salt-and-pepper frizzy hair. His T-shirt rode high, his pants rode low, and a thick waist and the upper portion of a large, fleshy butt were exposed for all the world to see. Yuck! Why do men do that? Letters on the back of his T-shirt spelled GWFITU.

The Greater Wilmington Film Industry Technicians' Union was a fairly new labor organization that was attempting to gain a toehold in North Carolina's "right to work" labor market. So Down East Productions was a union shop, I mused. Daddy had always argued that "right to work" translated into the right not to be paid competitive wages. Available nonunion, skilled and talented crews meant cheap labor for North Carolina's growing film industry that attracted major motion pictures formerly filmed in pricey Hollywood.

From the sublime to the ridiculous, I thought, as under brilliant lights, Mirabelle painstakingly glued cranberries to a white foam wreath form. Hundreds of cranberries filled an enormous clay bowl. With deft fingers she arranged the berries in concentric circles, but many rolled off the table, plopping onto the floor where they splattered or were crushed under her boots. As she worked, her low, hypnotic voice droned on, and my mind wandered.

Sadly, I recalled my conversation with Melanie the

night before and how I'd been forced to agree that it was time to consider a nursing home for Mama. I wanted to tell Jon about it, but hadn't yet got the chance.

The music swelled and brought me around. Mirabelle was saying, "With a little patience, you too can make this festive, all natural wreath for your front door." Smiling broadly, she held her creation aloft in front of the cameras.

"Cut!" a voice shouted. "Good show, Mirabelle."

"Styrofoam is a natural product?" Jon joked.

I shook my head. "Imagine what that wreath will look like when the birds get through pecking it."

Mirabelle stepped briskly off the stage. "That went well, don't you think?" Of course, no one dared disagree with her.

"Where is that good-for-nothing?" Raising her voice, she bellowed, "Teddy! Teddy Lambston!"

"I'm here, Mirabelle," Teddy shouted, hopping over cables as he scurried toward us from the dusky recesses of the immense studio.

"'I'm here, Mirabelle,'" she mimicked. "I thought I told you to stay put when I'm on the set! Now take care of that." She pointed to the kitchen floor and the smashed cranberries that puddled like fresh blood.

Teddy looked mortified as he hustled to the set. I wanted to reach out and pat him on the back. He didn't deserve this kind of treatment. And neither did I.

Mirabelle stomped off to her office. "Uh-oh. Trouble in paradise," Jon whispered, as we dragged our feet, postponing the moment when ours would be the heads on the chopping block.

"She's sharpening her ax," I whispered back.

"You mean her tongue, don't you?"

Mirabelle's office wasn't much more than a cubicle. She plopped down in her desk chair and groaned dramatically. "I have to do everything around here. I thought that little twerp was going to be a help."

Jon and I were not offered seats. I slipped into the one available chair that was wedged between the wall and the front of Mirabelle's desk. I was growing immune to her rude manners. I looked around at the small, cramped space she'd been assigned and realized she needed us as much as we needed her.

But Mirabelle was way too insensitive to ever acknowledge this fact even to herself. She snapped her fingers in my face. "All right, let's see them."

Boy, would I love to slap her silly, I thought. I unzipped my portfolio and pulled out a sheaf of pencil drawings that I'd tinted with watercolors. Jon leaned over Mirabelle's desk, removed a rubber band from the blueprints we'd finalized at Roy's Restaurant last evening and started to unroll them.

Mirabelle batted them away. "Not the blueprints."

Jon reared back, eyebrows raised.

Is she on something? I asked myself.

"I can't be bothered trying to decipher those hieroglyphics. Just make sure the place is structurally sound if you want to keep working in this town. Spare me the boring details."

Out of her line of sight, Jon grabbed his throat with both hands, lolled his tongue and rolled his eyes back, pretending he was hanging himself. I had to bite the insides of my cheeks to keep from laughing.

I spread my drawings on her desk, wondering if they'd get swatted away too. "As agreed, we're tearing down the walls that cut up the kitchen wing. Willie and his crew are breaking through the dumbwaiter shaft right now."

"Who's supervising him?" Mirabelle asked, leaning forward on her elbows and staring at my drawings. She tugged on her bangs in an agitated manner.

I shot a glance at Jon. "Willie's a reputable contractor, Mirabelle. He's been in business for forty years. He doesn't require supervision. I've been to the site this morning and the work is proceeding according to schedule."

"The site! The site! How many times do I have to tell you it's my house! Stop calling it a damned site!" I could feel my eyes grow wide. She was headed for a breakdown. There was nothing to say.

"And," she continued, working herself up to a hissy fit, "the work had better proceed on schedule with all the money I'm spending. You have to watch them every minute or they'll steal you blind."

All right, let's get this meeting back on track. "Are you finished?" I asked with deadly contempt.

She glared at me.

I pointed to the top sketch. "We'll have the Jenn-Air range dropped into this center island. That way the cameras can roll around you and shoot what you're cooking from four angles. Two convection ovens will be set in the wall behind you. It's the arrangement Julia Child had in her TV kitchen and it worked well."

"Julia Child, you say?" Mirabelle asked, perking up. "And the range is gas, not electric?"

"Yes. It will be a gas range," I assured her.

"Because I detest electric stoves."

"We've been through this before, Mirabelle. The stove will be gas. Now, may I continue?"

"Don't you get on your high horse with me, Ashley Wilkes!"

I ignored her outburst. "Above the island we'll hang a rack of shiny copper pots."

"No!" Mirabelle slapped the desk with the flat of her hand so hard I jumped. "No hanging pots over my head. They'll just be in the way and block the camera's view of my hair."

Well, that'd be an improvement! She's as crazy as a loon. I took one look at her shaggy hair and thought how much better shiny copper pots would look. "But they'll be way above your head."

"I said no."

"OK, Mirabelle, it's your kitchen…"

"And don't you forget it."

"Whatever you say. No hanging pots. Next. The counter top surrounding the Jenn-Air will be made of tiger maple which is a wonderfully stable hardwood that doesn't warp. I've put a double sink over here on the side so that…"

Behind me, a commotion erupted at the door as two men shouldered their way into the tiny space. The first man pressed inside, the second blocked the doorway, keeping others out or us in, I didn't know which. Trapped in the crush, I thought there wouldn't be enough air for us to breathe.

Both men looked like angry gangsters. Then I recognized the man in the doorway as my cameraman friend with the droopy trousers.

The first man yelled, "I just found out what you're doing, Mirabelle, and you won't get away with it!"

The speaker of this threat pushed forward, up against my chair which was already wedged tight in the corner. Mirabelle's desk formed a barricade in front of me and I was trapped.

Mirabelle jumped up. "Get out! Can't you see I'm in a meeting?"

"We're on to you. You're planning to take production out of this studio in December. You're gonna steal the bread out of my men's mouths. You…"

"Teddy, call Security!" Mirabelle shrieked.

Teddy? Was he here too? I couldn't see him. Jon was squeezed against the wall, looking miserable.

I looked up at wobbling, double chins. "Excuse me. Could I please get out."

Either he didn't hear me or he was maliciously blocking my way. He roared at Mirabelle, "The show's being syndicated by *Lifetime* Television and you're going to hire your own crew to tech it. And my union guys are out of jobs."

The union organizer was so close I could smell his sweat. His bulky body confined mine hotly. His chest, mere inches away, rumbled when he spoke. I craned my neck and tried to see his face but could only make out fat folds under his chin and a bright red neck.

"How long did you think you could keep your dirty little secret? We know you're building a studio out at your new house. That's why these folks are here!"

His pudgy fist clenched and unclenched close to my face. Surely he's not going to hit me, I thought as I took deep breaths. It's Mirabelle he's mad at. "Jon, get me out of here!" I shouted, but Jon was squeezed in as tightly as I. I couldn't help thinking that Detective Nicholas Yost would have cleared the room in a heartbeat.

Mirabelle leaned across the desk and pushed her face right up into the union leader's. "Leave my office this instant! You'll never work in this town again!"

Enough. I had to get out of here. "Let me out!" I made a fist and punched the fat man in his fat middle.

He didn't even flinch. He was staring at Mirabelle whose expression had turned triumphant. Fixing her gaze over the union leader's shoulder, she exclaimed, "Here come the troops!"

We're saved. I turned to see my rescuers, but the man's belly obstructed my view.

"Let'em come," he yelled. "We work here. We got every right to be here." But his belligerence had lost some of its sizzle. "Let me tell you a thing or two, Miss High and Mighty. You're chiseling my men out of a crack at crewing with a major network just so you can save a few measly bucks. Well, I'm calling a strike as of right now and your show's history, lady!"

Mirabelle's eyes widened and her mouth fell open. Her hand flew to her chest and pressed over her heart. "You can't do that! We have a contract. I'll sue!"

"Go ahead. Sue. We've got a contract too, and it says we get a six-month show. We're gonna get all the money you owe us. And when you move out to your fancy, schmancy studio—" and at this point he looked down and included me in his threat "—we'll be right outside. Anyone who crosses my picket line is dead meat!"

THIRTEEN

DETECTIVE YOST WAITED for me at a corner table in the Bridge Tender Restaurant. He'd telephoned late in the afternoon, and when I heard his officious tone I shuddered. He was in his cop mode, the frosty frosting to a truly wretched day.

After the guards had escorted the two union men out of Mirabelle's office, she absentmindedly granted approval of our plans with a wave of a hand. "Do whatever you like."

Uh-oh, this was not a good sign, I had thought. Whatever we did, she'd criticize, and might even refuse to pay.

"Here, just initial my drawing," I said.

She scribbled a hasty "MM" on the bottom of my sketch. Then she had stormed out, I guessed to meet with her lawyers about the brawl with the union leader.

Back at the site, or "Miss Mirabelle's manor house" as I had taken to calling it, I instructed the electricians to run cables in the kitchen according to the plans. I had ordered equipment from local suppliers who could deliver in days.

I worried about the complications a picket line might present for the project, yet some little part of me quivered with excitement that at long last someone was getting the better of Mirabelle Morgan. Someone was making her life as miserable as she had made others.

Now it seemed as if my day would end in yet another power struggle—this time with the wildly attractive yet imperious Detective Yost. All I wanted to do was go home and pull the covers over my head.

"There's an important matter we need to discuss," he had told me over the phone. "Could you meet me at the Bridge Tender Restaurant at six? We can talk over dinner." He was all business.

"Do I have a choice?" I asked, resenting the way he thought he could boss me around. Had I been crazy to think I was attracted to him?

"Of course, you have a choice, Ms. Wilkes, but our meeting is important to the outcome of this homicide. Further, it would be wise if you did not tell anyone you are meeting with me."

"I'm not at all tempted," I said through clenched teeth.

As I drove east on Oleander Drive, I reflected that the Bridge Tender Restaurant on the Intracoastal Waterway was a good choice for a clandestine meeting. Many of the clientele were tourists or wealthy yachtsmen who docked at the marina. Plus the cuisine was superb, and because of the brawl in Mirabelle's office and then my rush to get work rolling, I had skipped lunch.

"I appreciate your coming on such short notice, Ms. Wilkes," Detective Yost said, standing and pulling a chair out for me at a table in the corner overlooking the marina.

Well, this is more like it, I thought. He sounds almost

human. And he has good manners. As my eyes rested
on his face, I felt my resentment melt away. The day's
cares vanished as well. I couldn't help it, I liked the way
he looked. He seemed earnest, warm and considerate.
Despite his take-charge attitude, which I had to admit
was a quality I liked in a man and certainly was necessary for someone in law enforcement, he was pleasant
and seemed trustworthy, someone I'd like to know better. And there was that unmistakable chemistry between
us. Surely he felt it too.

"Call me Ashley," I said and extended my hand.

"And I'm Nick, Ashley." His handshake was warm and
dry, and he held on to my hand a tad longer than necessary.

"Nick," I said, liking the sound of his name.

The waiter arrived with a flourish of linen napkins
and water glasses, and recited the house specials. I ordered Maryland Crab Cakes. "Do you have Arbor Mist
Blackberry Merlot?" I asked.

The waiter practically sneered.

I have to confess to liking cheap wine. "OK, your
house Merlot then," I said.

Nick ordered Herb Crusted Grouper and seltzer
water with lime.

"You wanted to talk to me about the case," I prompted.

"Let's wait until the food comes so we won't be
interrupted. How's the restoration progressing? You look
tired."

"Thanks a lot. My day was miserable, if you must
know."

"I'm sorry. You look good. Just tired. Anything you want to talk about?"

"No. And I'm the one who's sorry. I shouldn't be complaining to you."

"Why not? I'm a good listener. Who's responsible for making you miserable?" The way he said that made me think he'd send out a squad of officers to pistol whip the offender.

I saw him differently then, as a person, an equal, not a detective who was complicating my life. His intriguing hazel eyes focused on me alone. They did not flit about the room in search of other women, loathsome treatment I'd endured from countless, thoughtless dates. Nick had a way of making me feel like I was the only woman in the room. I decided to take a chance and confide in him.

"My sister and I spent most of the afternoon looking at memory care facilities. We're going to have to institutionalize our mother because of her dementia. Her doctor has been recommending this confinement for some time, but I've been stalling. I see now that it's the right thing to do. Still, it's hard."

"I'm sorry, Ashley. I had to make the same decision about my dad last year, so I know what you're going through. I thought I could avoid committing him, that I'd be able to look after him myself, but then it got to the point where I had to admit his illness was more than I could handle. Keeping him with me wasn't fair to him. Still, I felt like a failure."

And you don't handle failure well, do you? I thought.

Well, neither do I. That makes two of us. "I know what you mean."

Nick continued, "Dad and I lived together in an old house in Carolina Heights so that made the separation even harder to handle. Now it's just me rattling around in that big house. I miss him—the man he used to be." The light in his eyes dimmed. "But my work keeps me busy so I'm not at home much."

"I appreciate your telling me. Was your dad a cop too?"

"No, an ER doc at the medical center before he got ill."

"Oh." Now I knew why his name was familiar. I had a feeling Detective Yost knew far more about me than I did about him. For starters, he probably knew all the details of my father's death, and that Daddy had been drinking.

I thought about Nick sharing a house with his father. "I'm not planning on moving into my mother's house," I told him. "My sister thinks we should sell it."

I recalled what Melanie said after our interview at the Magnolia Manor long-term care nursing facility. "That waterfront property will bring a couple of mil, easy."

How, I wondered, could Melanie relinquish our mother and our family home so easily? If I couldn't hold on to Mama, I at least wanted to hang on to our family home for a while. Yet, I acknowledged that it would have to be sold to pay Mama's medical bills.

"I know who your sister is. A sharp Realtor."

The waiter brought our food. My Merlot was slightly cooler than room temperature, just the way I liked it. "How's the grouper?" I asked as I cut into my crab cake with a fork.

"Perfect," he replied. "I like this place. I eat here often."

For a while, we ate in silence. I felt comfortable with him and with the silence.

Then Nick said, "Must be great living out here on the waterway. I've thought about selling my place and buying something out here." He smiled, showing those fatal dimples. "Actually, my dream is to live on a houseboat. Yet, that would mean that I've given up hope my dad will come home. I'm not ready to do that. Maybe they'll discover a miracle cure before it's too late for my dad and your mother." He shrugged magnificent shoulders. "I know it's not going to happen. He's never coming home."

We had something in common. I liked the way he expressed himself. I liked the way he looked. I liked the way he looked at me. I'm falling for this guy, I realized with a shock. I couldn't believe I was confiding in him, or that he was sharing his deepest feelings with me. I couldn't believe how much I liked him. But he's nice, I thought. He'd taken the trouble to shave and change into a fresh shirt. I liked a man who cared about his appearance.

He interrupted my musings. "I've decided to take you up on your offer to help with the investigation. What I want you to do is safe and simple, nothing risky. That is, if you still want to help."

Did I? There was no need for me to involve myself with a matter that might prove dangerous. Still, what better way to get an inside track on the police investigation and to learn what Nick knew. I did have a personal stake in the case: I was the one who discovered the skeletons. I felt possessive about Campbell House. And what a perfect excuse to see more of Nick.

"Sure. I'll be glad to help in any way I can. Have you identified the victims?"

He arched an eyebrow. He's used to being in charge. I suppressed a chuckle.

His cell phone chirped. "Excuse me. I've got to take this."

"Yost," he said into the phone. A few yeps followed, then, "Later."

"Sorry about that," he said to me. "Now where were we? Oh, yes. The murder victims. Guess it won't do any harm to tell you. That was my office. It'll be on the eleven o'clock news."

"You have identified them."

"Yes. Reggie and Shelby Campbell, the couple who owned the house."

"So Melanie was right."

"Well, that would be the obvious assumption, wouldn't it?"

"Are you sure?"

"We're sure. We were able to make positive identifications by comparing our dental X rays and bone X rays with those at a local dentist's office and with a sports medicine doctor."

I pushed my plate away, no longer hungry. I felt a sudden chill and gulped red wine, hoping it would warm me. The details of the case were grisly. Somehow hearing about the murders from the police perspective made them seem more real and menacing. Somewhere out there, a murderer was walking around scot-free, a killer who had gotten away with the savage murder of two of the town's wealthiest citizens. Was the motive robbery? Was the killer someone I knew? And how dangerous would he become when the police got close?

FOURTEEN

OUR TABLE OVERLOOKED the marina where yacht lights twinkled in the darkness like a swarm of lightning bugs. Across the channel, Blue Water Restaurant was lit up like a cruise ship.

"What else have you learned?" I asked.

He gave me a long, level look as if weighing how much he wanted to reveal.

"OK. We canvassed Orange Street. Lucky for us, most of the homeowners who lived there six years ago are still there today, although two people did die."

Noting my look of inquiry, he reassured me with, "Of natural causes."

"Go on. You learned something."

"Six years is a long time to remember the details of a particular night, that's why it's especially helpful that a neighbor, Ellen Burns, remembered seeing a man and woman leave Campbell House on a night in October six years ago. She thought the couple were Reggie and Shelby Campbell. That's what the killers wanted her to think and it worked."

"She told me," I said.

"She told you?"

"Yes, she came running over that morning before we

found the skeletons, and told me about how she was friends with Jean Campbell, and then after Jean's death, Reggie and Shelby kept her company, and how she was miffed that they took off without saying goodbye."

Nick scooted his chair in closer and leaned closer. "So none of this is news to you."

"Well, maybe not. Tell me what she said."

"That's she's an insomniac so she's up most nights. She roams around her garden in mild weather. On the night in question she was sitting in her front porch swing. She saw the lights in Campbell House go out. Then she saw a man and a woman leave the house, each carrying luggage which they deposited in the trunk of the Campbell car."

"But we know they were not the Campbells," I said.

"She admits she didn't see their faces, but she had no reason to suspect they were not the Campbells. When the trunk light went on, she caught glimpses of clothing Reggie and Shelby had been wearing earlier in the day. They both had on hats, which at the time she thought was odd because it was the middle of the night. Just as she was thinking she ought to cross the street and ask if they were leaving, they drove off."

"Hmmmm. Someone was very clever, Nick. I think they were people who knew the Campbells well. People who knew that Ellen Burns was an insomniac. They staged that departure for her sake, so she'd spread the story."

Nick explained, "So when she gets a postcard from London, signed 'Shelby,' and saying they had flown to London 'on a whim,' she spreads the story. She saved those postcards, and the first one said that the Campbells were visiting friends in England, then they planned to spend Christmas in Paris. They might return after the first of the year, or they might not. In the meantime, Mrs. Burns would see a caretaker on the property tending the garden and she should not be concerned."

I was about to blurt out that I'd met the caretaker but caught myself. "Have you questioned him?" I asked.

"We know who he is, and we're running him down. We'll find him."

"Teddy Lambston told me his mother got post-cards too."

"Most of the neighbors said they received postcards. Mrs. Burns gave us hers. We're having a handwriting expert look at them. Of course, they're forgeries, but if we get a suspect we can make a hand-writing comparison. Later, Mrs. Burns heard that the Campbells had decided to live in Europe permanently."

"Does she remember who told her that?"

"She said it was common knowledge."

"From what I hear they were eccentric." I thought about the wild parties Jon had told me about. "Well, that solves one mystery."

"What's that?"

"Why the front door key is missing."

Nick blinked, then gave me a sharp, penetrating stare. Well, that sure got him sipping my Kool Aid. "The front door key? Go on. Tell me about the front door key."

"The murderers used it to lock the door behind them when they left, then they took it with them."

Nick's cell phone chirped again. He grunted impatiently into it a few times before disconnecting. His face was closed up, guarded. "You never found the key?" His tone seemed indifferent, conversational. This must be the way he is when he interrogates suspects, I thought.

"No. We looked everywhere. All the other keys were there in the house. The killers took the front door key with them. Find that key and you'll find the killers."

The transformation was swift. Nick was back with me, beaming. "You'd make a good detective, Ashley."

I felt myself beam. Why did his opinion of me matter so much? "We're fitting the pieces together, Nick. But what about cause of death? Were they shot as you suspected?"

His hand inched toward mine on the table, then stopped. "Are you sure you want to hear this?"

"Yes. I'm involved in this case whether I want to be or not."

"That's true," he acknowledged. "But I never want you to do anything risky. Hearing the details from me, is one thing. Poking around on your own…well, just don't do it."

"Oh, no, I'd never do that," I said, with fingers crossed under the table.

"OK, here's what we know. Reggie was shot. The forensic anthropologist who examined the bones assured us that chips he found on Reggie's ribs were consistent with entry wounds caused by the .38 caliber bullets we found. The bullets had lodged inside his torso. Over the years they settled among the bones."

"Did Mrs. Burns hear gunshots?"

"You'd think she would have, but she says she didn't. She's a little hard of hearing…"

"Oh, yes, that's right…"

"…and those brick walls are as thick as a fortress. She might have been inside her own house when the shots were fired, and only came out on the porch later."

"What about Shelby? Was she shot too?"

"No, Ashley. Mrs. Campbell died of other causes. The anthropologist found multiple unhealed fractures, meaning they occurred at the time of death."

"What does that mean?"

"You sure you want to hear this?"

"Yes."

"Her skull was fractured, her neck was broken. She also had a broken right arm, right hand and foot."

My hand flew to my own neck. "How awful! Poor Shelby. Are you saying someone beat her to death?"

"Not beaten. Her injuries are consistent with a serious fall. We think she fell or was pushed down the stairs."

"Oh, no! That long staircase."

Nick took my hand in his. I looked into his eyes. They were warm and caring. He shared my concern. He was solid and reliable. He's everything I want, I thought.

"I'm sorry, Ashley, I've upset you, and that's the last thing I want to do."

"It's OK. It's not your fault. I insisted on knowing."

The waiter came up, presented us with the check. I reached for my wallet. "Put that away," Nick said. "I insist. I invited you. You're my guest."

"Well, thanks," I murmured.

He started to get up when I reminded him, "You said you needed my help. What do you want me to do? I'll help any way I can."

"Let's get out of here first. I'll walk you to your car. We'll talk outside." His hand felt warm on my back as we threaded our way among crowded tables.

Outside, a bracing coolness had spread over the coast. I stood with Nick at the edge of the crowded parking lot. Luxury automobiles filled every parking slip, except his and mine. The night was quite dark but lights from the marina danced on the water like a constellation of stars.

Nick moved close and his nearness took my breath away. "What do you want me to do?" My throat was dry, my voice husky. I wasn't even sure what I was asking.

He cleared his throat. I figured him for the sort who found it difficult to ask a favor. "Ashley, I know you're on the guest list for the benefit at Thalian Hall tomorrow night."

"You sure know a lot about me."

"Sorry. It just seems that way. I'd like to be your date for that party. If that's OK."

His date? My stomach turned flip-flops.

Nick explained in a rush. "As your date, I'll fit right in. The other guests won't question my being there. Maybe they'll stop thinking of me as a cop long enough to open up. I hope I'll learn something. Many of the people the Campbells socialized with will be at that party, and I'd like a chance to talk to them in a social setting. I think I'll learn something."

I opened my mouth to reply but his phone chirped again. He mumbled a few replies—I couldn't make out what—and ended with, "I'm on my way."

He disconnected, looked at me. "So what do you say? Will you let me take you?"

So that was what this evening had been about. That was why he was nice to me, so concerned about my problems with Mama. He's using me. What an idiot I am to think romance was happening between us.

I took a deep breath and pulled myself together before I could say something foolish. "Sure, Nick, we can do that."

He reached out a hand and placed it on my arm, gently. "I've upset you, Ashley. I'm sorry. I wish things could be different. But right now, this investigation is my top priority and you're the only person I can turn to."

"No explanations necessary, Detective Yost. You got what you came for. I'll meet you at the party at eight." I moved toward my car.

"No, Ashley. Wait!" He ran after me. "I'll pick you up. It's the least I can do."

FIFTEEN

I FELT WAY TOO FORLORN to face my empty house. I sat in my car for a moment, wondering what to do next. I watched Nick's car pull out of the lot, taillights winking as he merged with the traffic at the intersection of Eastwood Road.

Shelby Campbell had tumbled down the stairs to her death, before or after Reggie was shot. Nick said the news would be broadcast at eleven. I thought about Teddy. I couldn't let him hear about his friends' deaths from the TV news. He was going to be devastated. I wasn't a bit sleepy. I'd drive back into town and tell him myself. But first I had a stop to make.

I started the engine and turned onto Airlie Drive, heading in the opposite direction from home. I followed the waterway for a quarter mile until it curved inland. It was impossible for me to drive this route without feeling a tug on my heartstrings. This was where Daddy died.

I passed Airlie Gardens and Arboretum, closed now and shrouded in heavy darkness. Picking up Oleander Drive for a short hop, I crossed the bridge over Bradley Creek, then made a sharp left into the heavily wooded neighborhood at Greenville Loop Road. Melanie lived at the end of Rabbit Run on Sandpiper Cove in a ranch with bleached cedar shakes, green shutters, and a split rail fence covered with late-blooming rambling roses.

My headlights picked out the opening in the fence and I maneuvered my Volvo down her sloping, sandy driveway, parking behind her new SUV.

The Volvo station wagon I drive used to belong to Mama before she stopped driving. It had many miles left on it and served me well as a business van, transporting tools and equipment to the site. With my commission from Mirabelle, I'd be able to buy a real van.

Melanie's garage door was shut but light shone diffusely from the windows in the house. I took my purse and stepped carefully down illuminated shallow steps to Melanie's small front porch. Pressing the doorbell, I heard soft chimes play inside. I waited but she didn't come. Maybe she's in the shower, I thought. I'll give her a minute.

I gazed out over the porch rail into the dark backyard where the land dropped away into the cove. A lush harvest moon floated out of cloud cover. Lights from the Coast Guard Station on the southern tip of Wrightsville Beach flickered across the water. Here in the woods, away from streets and traffic, the wind sighed and stirred piles of leaves.

I gave the doorbell a final ring. The porch light sprang on and I blinked. At the same time Melanie flung open the door.

"OK, what…? Oh, Ashley, it's you. What on earth are you doing here?"

"I'll only stay a minute. I have something to give you."

She hesitated, then invited me in. As she tied the

sash of a peach satin kimono securely around her waist, she gave her disheveled hair a shake.

"Were you asleep?" My feet sank into thick carpet as I stepped inside the foyer.

Melanie caught sight of herself in a mirror over a console and took a moment to comb her hair with her fingers. "No, I wasn't asleep. You've caught me…at a bad time, is all."

"You mean you're not alone?" I whispered, glancing down the shadowy hall toward the master bedroom. Faint light shone from the bedroom, slanting in a wedge on the hall carpet which meant the door was ajar. I didn't want whoever was in there to hear our conversation so I moved away, toward the living room.

"Let's talk over here." I guided Melanie into the adjoining living room where one small lamp glowed.

The serene room was done in pale taupes and ivories with deft touches of peach and aqua. I remembered how we'd decorated this room together when I was home on a summer break. How much fun we'd had shopping for the wonderful art deco pieces that blended marvelously with the fat Thirties-style Tuxedo sofas and club chairs. How we'd selected the filmy linen panels that hung in deep folds across the sliding glass doors that led to the terrace.

"What is this all about? Why are you behaving so mysteriously?" she asked.

"Shhh. I have something that belongs to you." I pulled the tissue-wrapped cameo brooch from my purse and placed it in her hand.

She unwrapped the tissue paper. "What's this? You certainly are acting strange, even for you... Oh, my stars!"

For a split second, her face registered alarm, and some other emotion. Fear? Had I seen fear? Then her face clamped shut, and she regarded me defiantly. "Mama's been looking for this brooch. Where did you find it?"

"Not Mama. You. You'd better tell me the truth, Melanie."

Her chin shot up. "Mama lost it. And you know how she is."

I moved to the far side of the room, as far away as possible from the passageway to the bedrooms.

"Where did you find this?" she asked again.

"I didn't find it. Tommy did. It was wedged down in a sofa he's reupholstering for me. Shelby Campbell's sofa. So that brooch has been hidden there for the past six years. What I want to know is how it got there."

"How do I know? Maybe I dropped it when I was looking at the house."

"As fastidious as you are! You'd never sit on that dusty sofa. No, Melanie, you've got to do better."

"Well, then maybe I lost it when I went for tea," she said with a casual shrug. "You're making too much of this, Ashley. Drop it."

"I don't want to quarrel with you, Melanie. We've been getting along really well lately and I want to keep it that way." Still I had my answer. I'd seen the alarm on her face and that fleeting look of fear. "You've got it back now, that's all that matters, and no one's the wiser."

"Do you mean no one knows?"

"Tommy knows, naturally, because he found it. But he has no idea it was yours. And well, Jon knows because I told him but we can trust him."

We left it at that and said goodnight. I couldn't bring myself to tell her that Nick might have overheard me telling Jon about it.

I DROVE TO Orange Street, straight past the darkened Campbell House. Seeing it filled me with pride. My restoration. Mirabelle might own it, Mirabelle might live in it, but deep down, this was my house. I was leaving my mark on it, just as in the future I would leave my signature on many restored houses in the District.

On the next block, my headlights illuminated Teddy's modest but charming sunny yellow house. The gingerbread trim was painted white and gray. An authentic Victorian, it had a corner porch with a turret room above. Lights blazed from the first floor windows so I assumed Teddy was still up. It was not yet eleven. The doorbell was old-fashioned, the kind you had to twist; it buzzed loudly.

Teddy opened the door, a wallpaper scraper in one hand. He smiled broadly when he saw me. "Ashley, you came. Come on in and I'll show you what I'm doing. You'll be interested in this."

"Sorry, it's so late."

"It's not late. I'll be up for hours more."

I followed him into the dining room where he was scraping off layers of dull, faded wallpaper.

"Mother never had time to decorate our house, she was always so busy decorating her clients' houses."

"You know, Teddy, I tried calling your mother when I was at home over school breaks. I wanted to find out where you were, but I could never reach her."

"She worked hard. She was always busy." He brushed off his hands. "How about a glass of wine? Mother left a good supply."

"Thanks, but no. It's late and I've got to drive home. But you go ahead and have one if you want." I followed him back to the kitchen.

"Not without you. Anyway, I'm going to work on that wallpaper for another hour. Mother was so clever about money. There wasn't even a mortgage to pay off when she died."

I touched Teddy's shoulder. "I know you were proud of her."

Teddy lifted his chin. "I was. She was my best friend."

"What happened at the production studio after we left?" I asked, making conversation because I didn't want to spring the bad news on him.

"Didn't you hear, Ashley? Bob King and his crew made good on their threat to strike. Her show is off the air."

"You mean, they really did it? Picket lines and all."

Teddy's eyes blazed with excitement. "Yep. No one will go near Mirabelle's set. Everything's shut down."

"But that means you're out of a job, Teddy. I'm so sorry."

"I'll find something else. It didn't turn out to be what I expected anyway."

"He really stood up to her," I said, impressed with Bob King. "He really did it."

Teddy's expression was grim. "He hates her, Ashley. I heard him say he'd like to kill her."

"He'll have to get in line," I joked, and we both laughed. "I could use a cup of tea."

"Sure. I'll boil some water."

I sat at the kitchen table and watched Teddy fill a tea-kettle. "I like what you're doing here," I said, taking in the kitchen. New, yellow floral wallpaper covered the walls. The trim was painted cream, and there were folded shutters at the windows.

Teddy was taking china cups and saucers from one of the glass-front cabinets. "Mother collected these."

"You have a green thumb," I said, admiring pots of herbs on windowsills and a ruffly fern hanging over the sink. "I was so sorry to hear that she'd passed. I hope she didn't suffer."

Teddy set the table with a blue-and-white Spode teapot and matching teacups. "A massive heart attack," he said. "She died very quickly. The doctor said she wouldn't have known what was happening."

"That's a blessing." I waited until he'd sipped some tea, hoping it would fortify him. "I'm afraid I have bad news for you, Teddy. It'll be on TV later and I didn't want you to hear about it that way."

His eyes widened. "What is it, Ashley? You're scaring me."

I told him the skeletons had been positively identified as Shelby and Reggie Campbell.

"No! There has to be a mistake." The teacup rattled against the saucer as he replaced it. He dropped his head into his hands.

I got up and went around the table to him, putting an arm around his shoulders. "I'm sorry, Teddy. I felt I had to tell you."

"You're a good friend, Ashley. Do you think it's true?"

"Yes, I do Teddy. The detective who told me was positive."

"So that's where they've been all these years. I can't believe it. But what about the postcards? Who sent them?"

"I guess it was the murderer. Do you know anyone who hated them enough to kill them? Everyone says they were very popular and had lots of friends."

Teddy's wet eyes met mine. "I know someone who was afraid of Reggie. Afraid enough to kill. His next door neighbor, Sherman Warner. Reggie had something on Sherman that would have ruined him. It has to be Sherman. There's no one else."

SIXTEEN

WHEN I DROVE TO Campbell House the next morning, I found work progressing rapidly. Plumbers, electricians, and carpenters were practically tripping over each other in their haste to get things done. After I verified that everyone was doing what he was supposed to, I joined Willie out on the back porch steps.

He greeted me heartily. "That detective was messing round here early this morning, Miz Wilkes."

"Detective Yost? And when are you going to start calling me Ashley?"

"When you start calling me Mr. Hudson."

I punched his upper arm lightly. "The detective, Mr. Hudson?"

"Yeah, Yost. That's the one."

"What did he want?"

"Asking about the missing key. Wanted to check the front door lock. Took all the keys and tried each one hisself. I told him he was wasting his time, that the key was gone."

"Don't let it bother you, he's just being thorough." He didn't take my word for it either, I thought. I lifted my face to the sun. "It's a nice day. I think I'll take a little walk."

"I gotta get back inside," Willie said, rising slowly.

"Gotta keep an eye on my crew. I got eight of 'em in there now. The work'll go fast. We'll meet that deadline, Miz Wilkes."

"Yes, we will, Mr. Hudson."

I walked east. The house on the corner, circa 1851, was one of the first Italianate style houses to be built in Wilmington. Sherman and Muffie Warner's house. Any other time I'd stop to admire the architectural details, but this morning there was too much on my mind.

An alley ran from the back of the Campbell property to the street around the corner. I crossed Orange and started back on the opposite side. Mrs. Burns's broad front porch looked out over the street. The house was closed up. I wondered if she was at home. I wondered if she had remembered any other details about that night. Probably she slept during the day because she couldn't sleep at night. Should I take a chance and knock on her door? Oh, why was I bothering with all this? So there'd been murders here six years ago. They had nothing to do with me. The restoration was going well. That's all I cared about. Let the police investigate the murders. That was their job.

Across the street, Campbell House was a beehive of activity, with workers making trips back and forth to their trucks or to the two constructions Dumpsters in the rear alley. The sounds of construction filled the morning, music to my ears.

NICK AND I TREATED each other with stiff courtesy as we drove to Thalian Hall that night. I stole quick glances at him. He looked handsome in a formal, navy suit.

He cleared his throat and said, "Ashley, I don't know what went wrong. I thought we got off to a good start. I want us to be friends. If I've offended you in some way, I apologize."

I decided to be straight with him. "I thought we were becoming friends too, Nick. Then I found out the real reason you befriended me was so you could use me tonight."

When we stopped at a traffic light on Market Street, he turned my way. "Ashley, you're the one who offered to help me investigate the murders. Remember?"

Well, yes, I had done that.

"I just took you up on your offer. I didn't have a hidden agenda when we were having dinner at the Bridge Tender." He gave me a smile. There were those cute dimples again. "I enjoyed being with you. No ulterior motive."

Everything he said was correct.

"I'd like to see you again. I'm off tomorrow afternoon. How about taking in Riverfest with me?"

I felt myself grin. "Sure. I'd like to."

"Good. Friends?"

"Friends."

The light turned green and we drove around the Kenan Memorial Fountain at Fifth and Market. "I want to explain. Ordinarily when I'm working a case like this, the investigation takes over my life. I can't separate my personal life from my work life. The job consumes me."

"I can understand that," I said. "I'm pretty consumed by my own work. It takes over my whole life too."

"Well, I'm ready to change all that. I'd like to have a personal life. I'd like to spend my days off with you."

"Oh," I said, surprised. "Sounds nice. I'll try not to be so sensitive, Nick."

He reached over and took my hand. "And I'll try to sharpen my relationship skills, Ashley."

THE FIRST TWO PEOPLE I spotted at the party were Melanie and Mirabelle. They were air kissing and admiring each other's outfits.

"Stunning!"

"Wherever did you find that divine creation?"

Nick whispered in my ear, "You look better than they do."

"Thanks, but this type of party isn't my thing. If we weren't raising money for the Historic Preservation Society, I'd be at home snuggled up with a good decorating magazine."

I was wearing a simple black cocktail dress with the ruby necklace and earrings Mama had given me. A *Star-News* photographer came around and snapped my picture. I planned to rent a lockbox at the bank and deposit the jewels in it. Another of Mama's eccentricities had been to keep priceless jewels in her dresser drawers like costume jewelry. We were lucky she'd never been robbed.

Everyone was talking about the murders. "How did it feel to find Shelby and Reggie like that?" someone had the nerve to ask me, and I turned away, pretending not to hear.

Then the curiosity seekers migrated to Mirabelle's side, inquiring if she wasn't afraid to live in a house where a murder had taken place. Mirabelle rolled her eyes, clearly annoyed that she had to deal with idiots. Didn't they know that sentimentality had no place in Mirabelle's emotional makeup? Mirabelle lapped up publicity.

Where's Jon? I wondered, searching the crowds for a glimpse of him. "Have you seen Jon?" I asked Nick.

"Haven't noticed him," he replied. "There's Warner. He keeps dodging my calls. Come on, introduce me."

As we approached Sherman and Muffie, I wondered if Teddy had told Nick that Sherman Warner had a reason to fear Reggie Campbell. What had Reggie known about Warner that was a threat to him?

I introduced Nick to Sherman. He'd already met Muffie when he questioned the residents of Orange Street, but Sherman had been in New York. Sherman was a real preppie type, very clean-cut looking. Short brown hair that grew straight up, the tips bleached blonde. Small, rimless glasses. A dark suit with a dark silk shirt. He didn't seem too happy to meet Nick, but what could he do but make nice? Sherman was a stock broker. Jon had told me that Sherman made frequent trips to New York because he was having an affair with a female broker there. Everyone knew but Muffie.

A former beauty queen, Muffie had spent her teen years making the rounds of the pageant circuit, beginning as a Miss Teen America runner-up, culminating as Miss North Carolina in the Miss America Beauty Pageant. She was striking in a starved, brittle sort of way.

To give Nick a chance to quiz Sherman, I pulled Muffie aside on the pretext of talking fashion. I started describing an outfit I'd found at an outlet store. That's all it took. Muffie itemized every article of clothing in her closet.

Sara Beth Franks came up to us, greeting Muffie with a hug and kiss. She gave me the cold shoulder. "Oh. It's you. Melanie's little sister. I heard you were back."

Sara Beth was someone Nick should meet. He didn't seem to be getting much out of Sherman, so I called to him, "Nick, come meet Sara Beth. She's a very talented artist."

Jon had said Sara Beth was a member of Reggie and Shelby's circle. After high school, she'd gone to Paris to study at the Sorbonne before returning to Wilmington to teach at UNCW.

Sherman seized his chance to get away from Nick, grabbed Muffie's hand and steered her off.

I slipped away too, giving Nick and Sara Beth a chance to talk. Cocktails were being served in the Parquet Lobby outside the main theatre. Taking a glass of champagne, I slipped into the old part of the theatre. Here an anteroom was furnished with white wicker furniture under the original hand-painted canvas drop curtain portraying the "Isles of Greece." Thalian Hall dated from the Civil War.

As a season ticket holder, I regularly attended the traveling road shows and local little theatre productions that were such hits here. I paused to study photographs of Lillian Russell, Buffalo Bill Cody, John Phillip Sousa—celebrated performers who had starred at the Thalian.

I wondered if Sherman had been Reggie Campbell's broker? If he had been, surely he'd have known that Reggie was missing. No wonder Teddy accused him. Money was involved.

What had become of the Campbell fortune? Reggie's father had inherited a fortune from his father. Everyone knew Reggie was rich. How was it that no one noticed Reggie and Shelby had stopped spending money? Surely the detectives were following the money trail.

I looked around for Gordon and Cecily Cushman but didn't see them. They were another couple Nick needed to talk to.

As I was examining Edwin Booth's portrait, Sara Beth Franks joined me. "I don't appreciate your siccing that detective on us, Ashley. You always were too nosey for your own good, hanging around Melanie and all of us when you were little."

I stared her down. "Whether you appreciate it or not, Sara Beth, someone killed Reggie and Shelby. Nick's investigating and he's got a right to ask questions."

I expected another insult, instead tears sprang into Sara Beth's eyes and she turned and fled. Now what was that all about? These people bewildered me. I should have stayed at home. I knew that coming here was a mistake. All anyone wanted to talk about was the murders and how I'd discovered the remains.

I opened the Parquet Lobby door and escaped into the shadowy theater. The door did not close properly; it was warped. What an unpleasant person Sara Beth had become. The many loud voices were giving me a headache. As soon as I could manage it, I was out of here, I promised myself. Yet, in the empty theatre, the noisy chatter was muffled by the thick door even if it did not fit snugly. I sipped champagne and looked around.

I loved this beautiful old theatre. Thalian Hall has its share of ghosts too. Three thespians. It was common knowledge they were shy. They wouldn't show themselves tonight. The noisy crowd had sent them into hiding just as it had me.

OK, Wilkes, I told myself sternly, face the real reason you're not enjoying yourself tonight! Tomorrow, you and Melanie are moving Mama into Magnolia Manor. As soon as I could get away, I'd stop by her house, help Nellie tuck her in. Poor Mama, she didn't know it was the last time she'd be sleeping in her own bed.

I let my gaze wander over the architecture. The proscenium arch gleamed richly with ornate gold-leaf carvings. The kidney-shaped first gallery offered exceptional views of the stage. My eye traveled from painted friezes and murals to fluted pilasters with gilt capitals that supported the domed ceiling.

The house lights were dim, enhancing the rococo splendor. On the stage, musicians were assembling, snapping on reading lamps, tuning instruments. Later, we would be treated to show tunes from the best Broadway musicals.

Behind me, the door bumped. Uh-oh, was someone coming in? I moved into the back row and sat down in the aisle seat.

Outside the door, a man and woman quarreled. Shamelessly, I tilted my head toward the crack in the door.

"This is no time to pull out! Not with the expenses I'm incurring on that house."

I'd know that overbearing voice anywhere.

"I'm in way over my head, Mirabelle," a man said. "You've got to listen. I've already lost more money than I can afford on your schemes."

Who was that? I peered through the crack but only saw a dark suit and the back of a man's head.

"They are not schemes!" Mirabelle hissed. "A product line is just the next logical step in my plan. It's a money-maker. Guaranteed."

"Guaranteed? Sure, you're planning to build an empire but I'm the one putting up the money. And it's not even mine, it's Cecily's. Why don't you use your own money if this product line is such a sure thing?"

Cecily? Gordon?

"Don't you dare take that tone with me, Gordon Cushman. You know my money's all tied up in that house."

Gordon Cushman! And Mirabelle? Oh ho!

"That was a mistake. That house is bad luck. Just see what happened to Reggie and Shelby. And people are saying it's haunted."

"And that works to my advantage, Gordon darling. Nothing intrigues people like a haunted house. Buying that house was one of the smartest moves I ever made. My show is going national and it's crucial that it be telecast from the perfect setting. Martha Stewart tapes her shows from Turkey Hill Farm in Westport and her house is a lot older than mine. Don't tell me no one ever died in it!"

"Died maybe. But murdered?"

"Well, when my house is finished, it'll make her drafty shack look like an outhouse. My ratings will sky-rocket. Then I'll be offered product endorsements and that's when the money gets big. I envision Wal-Mart giving me a line of sheets and towels, paint, that sort of thing. Besides, the costs of fixing up the house are tax deductible. I thought you believed in me, Gordie, sweetie. Stick with me just a little longer. I'll make you rich, filthy, filthy rich. You'll see."

Gordon sighed deeply. "Cecily is getting suspicious."

"She should be suspicious," Mirabelle murmured huskily.

The door banged as Mirabelle pressed against her man.

"Not here. Cecily's around somewhere."

"No, she's not. She went upstairs with her gal pal Muffie."

Gordon groaned. "Mirabelle, stop! Cecily's asking questions about the money. She wants to know where it's invested and why we aren't getting a return on it."

"You'll think of some excuse to pacify her, my love. You always do. Darling, be a dear and be patient for just a little longer. Then you'll get all your money back plus heaps of interest."

"That's not good enough, Mirabelle. I'm sorry to put you in a bind, but it can't be helped. You've got to repay me now. I've got my own problems. Besides, Cecily earned that money. I never should have loaned it to you."

"Well, you can't have it now. It's tied up and there's no way I can get it out."

"Then you give me no choice, Mirabelle. I have to call my note. You do remember that you signed a note, don't you? Well, I'm calling it!"

"Oh, I don't think you'll do that, darling," Mirabelle said with saccharine sweetness. "You wouldn't want your precious Cecily to know that you gave me an unsecured loan for a half million dollars, would you?"

"You're threatening to destroy my marriage?"

"I wouldn't put it that way, darling. Let's just say I'm protecting my interests."

"I'd like to slap that smirk off your face."

"Why not kiss it off, Gordon darling." Mirabelle laughed suggestively, and pressed against him again.

He pushed her away. "Our affair was a mistake. I love my wife. She's been hurt once because of my weakness. I won't let you hurt her again."

"How touching. Where are the violins?"

"Be careful, Mirabelle. I won't let you destroy my marriage. And I want my money. Now, step aside and let me pass!"

Gordon Cushman, another member of the Campbells' inner circle.

SEVENTEEN

I COUNTED TO TEN then pushed the door open and left the dim theatre. Gordon and Mirabelle were no where in sight. That Mirabelle was a steel magnolia of the worse sort. Why, she was blackmailing Gordon.

As I maneuvered through the crowd, someone called my name and grabbed my hand. Betty Matthews, one of my favorite people, a community leader, president of the Historic Preservation Society.

"Ashley, I've been looking all over for you. Come, sit here with me." She patted the spot beside her on the round velvet "pouffe" that dated from 1900.

Betty was naturally elegant, with ash-blonde hair that she wore swept gracefully off her face. Her bones were good and her skin was tanned from days on the beach. Smile lines creased the outer corners of her pale gray eyes.

"Hi," I said, joining her. Betty is always sunny and optimistic, nothing seems to get her down. She usually cheers me up. "Looks like we're sold out tonight. The Society's treasury will certainly benefit from this turnout."

"Sure enough," Betty agreed. "I couldn't be more pleased. We should make enough to replenish the coffers tonight."

She peered into my face. "Land sakes, girl, how are you holding up? How dreadful for you to be the one to find those skeletons. Now, you must persevere and not let anything interfere with the restoration of Campbell House. Why, I've told everyone in town how much faith I have in your ability to restore the mansion to its former glory. I just know you'll do us proud. Campbell House will be the showplace of Wilmington again."

"Thanks, Betty. Having your support means a lot to me."

She patted my hand. "You have that. In abundance. I know Mirabelle isn't the easiest person to get along with. She's had a run-in with just about everyone in town. That woman's got more enemies than friends."

"So I hear."

"Well, I surely hope she doesn't plan to change the name of Campbell House to Morgan House," Betty said.

I chuckled. "I've already applied for a plaque from the historic foundation, so it won't do her any good if she tries."

"Good thinking, Ashley."

"I've got to go find my escort," I said, getting up.

"If you're referring to that nice young detective I saw you with earlier, I last spotted him upstairs in the ballroom where the caterers are serving supper."

I left Betty and went out into the lobby, then took the carpeted staircase that led to the ballroom on the mezzanine level.

"Ashley!" Someone caught my arm in the upper hallway.

I turned to see Cecily Cushman, our famous true-crime writer. Cecily had snow-white hair that fell to her shoulders, olive skin, black eyes and eyebrows. Arty looking. She always had little half glasses perched on her nose as though she was about to read fine print.

"You are just the person I want to talk to, Ashley," she said, eyeing me over the glasses. "My editor called me as soon as news of your discovery hit the wire services. My publishing house wants to do a book on the murders and they want me to write it."

"But the crime hasn't been solved," I protested.

She waved a hand dismissively. "Doesn't matter. We can do it as an unsolved case. Those are fascinatin' too. And I'll do some prying. Who knows? I may solve it myself. In any case, I'll do a lot of background stuff on Reggie and Shelby's lifestyle, the history of the Campbells all the way back to the Dark Ages, and then how you found that skull. Was it his or hers? No one has said."

I glared at her, shocked and disbelieving. "This conversation is making me ill and I was just about to have supper," I snapped, and left her standing there, mouth gaping open. I glanced back but she just gave me a smugly challenging look.

In the red carpeted ballroom, restaurants from Lumina Station had set up food on long tables. I filled a buffet platter with pasta and a sampling of toppings. Nick was already seated at one of the round tables. Jon was with him and seemed agitated, waving his hands about. Now what?

Curious, I started toward them, turning so suddenly I bumped into a large man.

"Oh!" I gasped, tightening my grip on my plate. It tilted precariously, threatening to spill tomato sauce on the man's dazzling white shirtfront that stretched snugly over his round belly. I stepped back, averting disaster. "I'm so sorry. Are you all right?"

"No harm done," the man said kindly. "It was my fault. I wasn't looking where I was going. My wife tells me I'm the original bull in a china shop."

He did look rather like a bull with his massive head and multiple chins. In fact, there was something oddly familiar about him. I transferred my plate to my left hand and extended my right. "Don't I know you? I'm Ashley Wilkes."

"Yes, Miss Wilkes, I know who you are although we haven't been formally introduced." He took the hand I offered, giving it a bone-crushing handshake.

I jerked my hand away. He seemed not to notice.

"I'm glad for a chance to speak to you, Miss Wilkes," he was saying. "I owe you an apology. I'm Bob King, head of the technicians' union."

Uh-oh. Yesterday morning in Mirabelle's office. Involuntarily, I took a step backward.

He made an embarrassed tittering noise. "I don't blame you for reacting that way. I was way out of line the way I treated you and Mr. Campbell. My gripe's not with you folks. I hope you'll accept my apology."

"Of course, Mr. King, think nothing of it." I backed away.

"But that woman you're working for, she's ruthless. She doesn't care how many people she hurts—just so she gets what she wants." A bright red stain spread over his neck and cheeks.

Behind me, a woman laughed, high and piercing. I glanced over my shoulder. Melanie. Her face was flushed and she was hanging on a man's arm. She laughed up into his face. He was a good head taller than she, even in her high heels. He slipped his arm around her waist to steady her. Was she drunk?

I tuned in what King was saying, "Your dad had a lot of friends in this town, Ms. Wilkes. I like to think I was one of them. That makes my treatment of you yesterday all the more inexcusable. It's just that she makes me furious. She doesn't care about anyone but herself. My guys have served her well. They make her look good, even when she makes stupid mistakes. And they've had to put up with a lot of crap from her!"

I edged further away. King seemed oblivious as he continued ranting. "She has no scruples, that woman. Thinks nothing of breaking our contract. She'll hire her own technicians to save a few measly bucks. Does she care that my men have families to feed?"

King was out of control just as he had been yesterday in Mirabelle's office. The man had a dangerous temper. All around us people stopped talking to stare at him.

"Yes, well, I am sorry for your predicament, Mr. King…"

"Well, I've fixed her. *Southern Style* wasn't filmed today. Cancelled. If I have my way, that woman will never be on television again."

"Well, at least you have that option," I said, attempting to mollify him. "I'm here with a detective," I said, pointing to Nick who'd heard the commotion and was bolting toward me.

King wasn't listening. He clenched and unclenched his large fists, just as he had yesterday morning. "Someday that woman's going to get what she deserves!"

EIGHTEEN

AT SEVEN O'CLOCK ON Saturday morning the thermometer on my porch registered a cool fifty-eight degrees. Stiff breezes blew off the waterway, and I experienced a pleasurable foretaste of the mild winters we get here on the coast. Dressed in khakis and a cotton sweater, I got into the station wagon, backed out onto Summer Rest Road, took Eastwood until it changed into Martin Luther King expressway and headed downtown to Orange Street. I wanted to check on the house then return home to spend the morning with Mama. We weren't able to manage a conversation, but we could hold hands and listen to music together. After lunch, Melanie and I were moving her to Magnolia Manor.

As I drove away from the coast with the sun at my back I thought about the scene Bob King had caused last night. Nick had stepped between me and the union leader, then handed me off to Jon. Nick got King to calm down, told everyone to go back to having a good time. He found King's wife and suggested she take her husband home. Then he asked Jon to drive me home, kissed me on the cheek goodnight, and said he had to get to headquarters. Jon lit up like a Christmas tree at the prospect of driving me home and I remembered how he had asked if we could date.

Melanie had rushed to my side. She'd introduced me to her client, who was also her date. Joel Fox, a former motion picture producer from Los Angeles, was scouting the Wilmington area for property to develop. There was something slick and oily about Fox that I did not like.

King was sure a scary guy. And Mirabelle was having an affair with Gordon Cushman. Gordon and his wife Cecily lived on Orange Street, had been part of the Campbell crowd. I wondered if Mirabelle had been part of that crowd too.

I had promised Nick I'd go to Riverfest with him later that afternoon. Should I tell him about Gordon's affair with Mirabelle, or would that just seem like gossip? Maybe I should just cancel; I wasn't much in the mood for a street fair.

I parked at the curb in front of Campbell House. The sounds of hammering, sawing, and scraping flowed through the open doors and windows. In two days, Willie had broken through the dumbwaiter shaft and floored over the chase. When I looked in the kitchen, three men wearing masks and eye shields were scraping cracked and peeling paint off the walls and trim.

Already new kitchen equipment and stock cabinets had been delivered. They were still packed in boxes, stored in the dining room. I walked through the shoulder-high aisles they formed, noting labels and reviewing a clipboard on which I'd checked off itemized equipment and supplies. Much as I would have preferred, there simply wasn't time to have custom cabinets built.

Willie stuck his head in the dining room. "Hey, Miz Wilkes."

"Hi, Willie. We're making good progress. I see the bricklayer is here."

"Yeah, got him in there stackin' the brickwork around the fireplace. I'm usin' that old brick like you said so the wall will have a nice antique look."

"That's great, Willie. Things are really moving along."

"Goin' good, Miz Wilkes. Let's just pray we don't find no more…uh, surprises."

"Amen to that."

I went down to the basement to make another tour of that level. High windows were still boarded up because a few glass panes were broken and we were too busy with the kitchen to get to them. I snapped on lights as I went from room to room. Mostly they were storerooms, and a kind of scullery that in the old days had served the kitchen on the first floor. The dumbwaiter originated here behind a door set waist high in the wall. The shaft was now sealed over on the first floor level.

A stone sink and oak cupboards lined the walls. A water mark from long ago flooding made a chalky line. We were too far above sea level for the river to rise this high but once every decade or so, heavy storm surges filled streets and basements and the network of underground tunnels upon which downtown was built.

Dark, low-ceilinged rooms connected one to another like freight train cars. Dusty and draped with spider webs, they were ghostly reminders of the days of plentiful servants.

I pulled open stuck cabinet doors, poking around for anything useful. A possible treasure? Someone had left some tools behind, a hammer, a screwdriver, wads of twine. The glass in the old wall cabinet doors was hand-blown, blurry with a faint bluish tint. Inspiration struck. I would find a place for these old cabinets in the new kitchen, maybe attach them to the brick wall and display china and glassware in them. They'd add an antique flavor I'd never be able to duplicate with new cabinets.

Touring the other rooms, which included the original laundry, an empty wine cellar, and an empty but still sooty coal room, I continued to search for other treasures I might use upstairs. I found antique hardware and doorknobs, and old wooden Venetian blinds wrapped in newspaper that dated from the Thirties. I returned to the first floor.

I had always loved this house. Even before I'd seen the inside when it was on the Olde Wilmington by Candlelight Tour, I used to stand outside the fence and admire it. It was houses like this that had inspired me to study historic preservation.

The great hall was about twenty feet long by thirteen feet wide. The floor was made of beautiful inlaid marble, the walls were painted, and I was hoping to uncover a hand-painted mural or some other gem once restoration moved into the front rooms. My footsteps echoed eerily. I stood at the bottom of the staircase and looked up. The stairs curved gently up to the second floor, but they were steep and the treads were shallow. No carpeting. A fall on those steps could be fatal.

I pictured Shelby Campbell the last time I had seen her at the Christmas ball. She'd been wearing a shimmering blue ball gown. She was petite and delicate, and with her long yellow hair she'd looked like Cinderella at the ball.

I jumped with a start as I realized something important. On the night she died, Shelby had been naked. I'd watched the recovery of the skeletons through my peephole long enough to know that no fabric remnants had been found. Shelby's and Reggie's clothing had either been removed by the killers before the bodies were hidden, or they were naked when they were killed.

I pictured Shelby fleeing from the killer. She had run to the stairs, started down, then lost her balance. My arms flew out as if to catch her.

On the steep, polished stairs, she would have tumbled fast. I could almost hear the thud as her skull cracked against the wall.

At that point she would have been mercifully unconscious. Her limp body would have careened off the hard surfaces until she reached the bottom where I stood. She had pitched forward onto the marble floor, twisting and breaking her neck, landing so violently on her right arm, hand, and foot, they were broken under her weight.

I was shivering, hugging my arms, my teeth chattering. I saw how it had happened. Bile pushed up, burning the back of my throat. Poor Shelby. What atrocity had taken place here on that night so long ago? Who had frightened her so badly she'd pitched headlong down the stairs to her death? Or had she been pushed? One thing was clear, I was identifying with Shelby just as I'd always identified with her house. I wanted her killer found and brought to justice. I wouldn't rest until I knew the truth.

NINETEEN

WE DROVE MAMA TO Magnolia Manor after lunch. At first she seemed withdrawn and meek, but when she saw the large white house with the white columns, she breathed a happy, "Tara!" and relaxed. We settled her in her room which she seemed to like until the manager encouraged us to leave so Mama could join a pottery painting class.

Melanie dropped me at my cottage, but one glance at Mama's empty house next door and I knew I had to get away. Not even bothering to run inside to check my answering machine, I backed the station wagon off the brick pavers and headed back to Campbell House. Work was the answer. I called Nick from my car and asked to be excused from our Riverfest date. "I'm not in the mood for a street festival."

"I know what you're going through," he said. "I've been there, remember? You have to keep busy, keep going, get on with your own life. It's what your mother would want for you if she were her old self."

"All I know is that I feel guilty. Like I've really let her down."

"Don't, Ashley."

"But she seemed so confused, Nick."

"Ashley, I'm not saying this to make you feel better. After a few days, she'll feel safer there, and that will be comfort to her and to you."

"I hope you're right. OK, I'll see you in a while. Pick me up at Campbell House."

I pulled into Orange Street. A silver-colored Mercedes was parked under the trees in front of Campbell House. I park behind it, recognizing it at once. I shouldn't have been surprised that Mirabelle had come here. With her television show off the air, what else did she have to do but micromanage the restoration project? Besides, she was bound to show up sooner or later. I steeled myself for another of her irrational outbursts.

"Why was the front door standing open for all the world to come and go?" she demanded as soon as she saw me. She was dressed in jeans and boots with a denim shirt.

Foam peanuts and plastic bubble wrap flew from her hands as she dug furiously in a box like a dog digging for a bone. She looked up at me and frowned.

Trying to gain some control of the situation, I asked, "Do you like what we've accomplished so far?"

"How can I tell in this mess?"

We locked eyes over wooden crates and large cardboard boxes. I was the first to break eye contact. The sounds of construction came from the kitchen. A draft flowed through the house, causing the chandelier crystals to dance crazily and tinkle like water falling.

"Come on back to the kitchen, Mirabelle, and I'll

explain what we're doing and how everything will look when we're done."

"Not now. I'm checking that those people sent the right cookware. You can't trust anyone these days and you're a fool if you do."

She retrieved a Swiss Army knife from the brown leather shoulder bag that was propped on one of the boxes. I watched as she sliced efficiently through the flaps of a second box. "Oh, here are my German carbon steel knives. They'd better be the sizes I ordered."

I looked around helplessly. I'd had the Sheraton dining room furniture sent to an expert for repairs and cleaning. The electricity to the chandelier had been disconnected until an electrician could make repairs. In the corners, curved paneled doors concealed small storage compartments. One door led to a butler's pantry and the kitchen wing. Pale green light filtered through tall windows from the jungle outside.

"I've contacted Gilbert's Nursery and they're sending a crew out next week to prune the trees and shrubbery."

"Gilbert's?" Mirabelle repeated vaguely. "Oh, well, cancel them, dear. I've already made arrangements for the landscaping."

"You have? But that's my job. That's what you hired me to do. You shouldn't make other arrangements without consulting me."

"Consulting you!" She waved the army knife, then slashed through the top of a rectangular box. Straightening up, she fixed me with an exasperated expression.

"Consult you, indeed. Ray Woods is doing the work as a favor to me."

"Ray Woods? But he's a novice, Mirabelle. He's never handled a job of this magnitude or importance. And what do you mean 'as a favor'? Are you saying he's not charging a fee?"

I couldn't believe how Mirabelle was wresting control of the project right out of my hands. My pulse banged in my temples and my head was starting to ache.

Mirabelle tossed the army knife on top of the box and jammed her fists on her hips. "You are such a Girl Scout, Ashley Wilkes. You know nothing about negotiating or making things happen. Ray will do all the landscaping, including planting an herb garden for me next spring. In return, I'll feature his landscaping projects on my show."

Disapproval must have shown on my face because she said, "You'd better wise up, dear. This is the way the real world operates."

"SHE'S CHEATING ME out of my commission on landscaping," I complained to Nick. We glanced back at the house where she was standing in the door, watching us.

He put his arm around my shoulders and gave me an encouraging squeeze. "Come on. Let's forget about her and homicide cases and everything else for a couple of hours."

"You're on," I said, determined to have a good time.

Leaves fluttered from the trees, weightless as feathers, then settled at our feet as we strolled leisurely toward the river. Autumn. My favorite season. But autumn on the coast meant hurricanes. Today, though, the sky was crystal clear, true Carolina blue. Soft breezes sent piles of leaves swirling.

"Don't let her get you down, Ashley. There'll be other clients once you've finished this house. Most of them will be nice people."

"You're right. I can't let her get to me."

At Third Street we passed the Zebulon Latimer House, circa 1852, an impressive Italianate structure where the Lower Cape Fear Historical Society had its headquarters.

The sounds of music and gaiety drifted our way as we joined the flow of pedestrians headed for the festival. A familiar couple came trudging up the hill, red baseball caps bobbing.

"Oh look, it's Sherman and Muffie Warner."

"He's been avoiding me," Nick said.

Sherman and Muffie were dressed alike in black Bermuda shorts, white Polo shirts, white socks with white Reeboks, and red baseball caps.

"You guys leaving already?" I called, my tone lightly affable.

The four of us merged on the sidewalk. Sherman seemed even less friendly than he had been last night. He kept moving, pulling Muffie with him.

"It's a mob scene," Muffie complained. Her blonde ponytail stuck out of the hole in the back of her cap. She had an expensive-looking camera slung over her shoulder.

"Yeah, there's a big crowd," Sherman grumbled, backing away. "Too many people for us. Anyway, we were there for hours. Looking forward to putting my feet up and having a drink."

Nick said to Sherman, "We didn't get a chance to finish our conversation last night, Warner. I still have a few questions. Mind if I call you at home later?"

Sherman tried for casual indifference, but his hostility cut through the air like a blade. "Does it make any difference if I do mind? Call whenever you like."

"Well, nice seeing you," I said as the Warners headed for home.

"What's he so upset about?" I asked Nick. I remembered Teddy pointing the finger at Sherman. "Does he have something to hide?" Before Nick could reply, I went on, "Oh, you know what occurred to me last night? Sherman and Reggie used to be friends. Maybe Sherman was Reggie's broker. Somebody had to be managing the Campbell fortune all these years."

"There is no fortune, Ashley."

I stopped abruptly. "What! That can't be. Everyone knows they're rich. Were rich."

"Maybe once, but not for a long time."

"But what happened to the money?"

"This is confidential information so you can't tell anyone. Promise me."

"Scout's honor."

"There was a safe deposit box at the bank containing stock certificates, and a little less than $20,000 in cash. The balance of their checking account was around $3,000."

"Twenty-three thousand dollars? That's all? What is the stock worth?"

"Worthless. Tech stocks that went belly-up years ago."

When the light changed, we crossed Front Street, dodging a group of happy, whooping children.

"Well, I just can't believe it. They owned that fabulous house." I pondered this incredible news for a minute. "I've got it! You have to pay a rental fee on a safe deposit box. So who's been paying that?"

Nick shook his head. "The bank drafted their checking account annually."

"And no one at the bank thought it was strange that in six years the only transactions on the account were drafts for a safe deposit box rental?"

"You'd be surprised at the number of inactive accounts the banks are holding."

"Well, I just don't understand how people can disappear for six years without someone noticing. What about the IRS? And the post office? What about their mail delivery?"

"We've looked into all that. Of course, no tax returns were filed. The IRS didn't pursue it because no earnings or W-2's had been reported. Stock hadn't been sold so there was no capital gain to report. Guess they really were as eccentric as everyone claims because they'd been living on cash."

I considered this news. If they'd been living on cash for a lot of years, that might explain why there was so little left.

Nick continued, "The mail that piled up at their house was returned to the post office by the mail carrier. The post office either returned it to the senders or forwarded it to the dead letter office. According to the letter carrier, very little first-class mail came."

"So our killer was really clever," I concluded. "Careful enough to pay property taxes. To lock all the doors and windows so no one could get inside and find the bodies. After six years, there wouldn't…" I paused.

"Be an odor?"

"Yes. Right. So it was OK to stop paying taxes and sending fake letters and postcards. If someone went inside the house, they wouldn't find anything."

"Our killer was pretty thorough," Nick said. "Had the water and electricity disconnected, and the telephone and cable service. Arranged for a caretaker to mow the lawn and secure the house from vandals."

So Nick knew about Henry.

"Yes," Nick continued, "he thought of everything. Except that someone might come along one day and want to remodel the kitchen and tear down some walls."

"And the killer traveled abroad to London and Paris and sent forged communications back home to friends and neighbors. Did you ask Sherman and Muffie if they got postcards too? And how about the Cushmans and Sara Beth Franks? Did they get postcards like everyone else?"

"A few at first. Then as the years went by, nothing. You know, people get busy with their own lives and lose track of time," Nick said thoughtfully. "Out of sight, out of mind. No one was counting the years."

"You can be sure the killer was," I said.

Nick continued, "The people I talked to told me they just assumed that one day Reggie and Shelby would turn up, open the house, and throw a big party. People I've questioned expressed surprise that six years had passed. They just weren't thinking about them."

TWENTY

NICK AND I ARRIVED AT Riverfest to the sound of music. Across from the Alton Lennon Federal Building, known to Andy Griffith fans as Matlock's courthouse, the Gospel Stage featured spiritual music. Cloggers were performing at the Cotton Exchange. A group called the Swingshift played on the Hilton stage. Bob King and his union technicians were monitoring sound equipment on the stage across from the Federal Building.

At Millie Prechtl's booth we bought steak and cheese sandwiches and "Millie's Original" funnel cakes. Carrying our food purchases and giant Cokes to a low wall on the esplanade, we squeezed in among a happy crowd. Everyone was having a good time.

Out on the Cape Fear, the Henrietta III paddle wheeler took visitors on an old-fashioned riverboat ride. Rowing clubs competed on the water.

"Oh, look, there's Teddy," I said. "I didn't know he could do that!"

Teddy Lambston was one of a troupe of jugglers. As he tossed his pins into the air, white ruffles fluttered around his wrists. I couldn't take my eyes off him, impressed by how effortlessly he kept the pins moving.

"Hi, Ashley," he called when the troupe took a break.

"Glad you came. Isn't this something? Remember those street fairs in New York? Especially that big festival in Little Italy?"

"I sure do. I especially liked the big fair on Second Avenue. My roommate and I never missed it. You know Detective Yost, don't you?"

Nick shook hands with Teddy. "Mr. Lambston was one of the first people I talked to when I canvassed Orange Street."

"Call me Teddy." He pulled out a folded tissue and wiped the perspiration that had collected under his bangs.

"We were wondering who all got the fake postcards," I said.

Teddy's face darkened. "All I know about is a few neighbors, and my mother. I started NYU that fall, but I saw the postcards when I came home for Christmas. Now, well, it's confusing. I can't get used to the idea that all this time Shelby and Reggie were actually dead. Are the police sure, Detective Yost? It couldn't be someone else?"

"We're sure, Mr. Lambston, and I'm sorry for your loss. Did your mother save any of those cards? It would help us to have them if they're still around."

"Oooh, you mean, there might be fingerprints. Gee, I don't know but I'll look for them. If I find them, I'll call you. I want you to catch whoever did this. Uh-oh, they're calling me. Gotta go. We're on again."

We watched the troupe perform for a few minutes, then wandered slowly through the crowd. At the promenade we leaned on the railing as the John Maffitt sailed by, ferrying groups across the river to the Battleship North Carolina.

Sara Beth Franks, the artist who had been Shelby and Reggie's friend, displayed her paintings along the stone wall. She was doing a brisk business. Sara Beth's seascapes and beach scenes were popular with decorators and other collectors.

A teenage artist, seated under a colorful umbrella, was drawing caricatures. I coaxed Nick into having his done, watching over the young artist's shoulder as with a few deft strokes he captured the real Nick, the man I saw when he wasn't "on the job."

I sensed a couple standing behind me and turned to see Gordon and Cecily Cushman. They said hello and I said, "Hi." After what I'd overheard last night, I wasn't able to look Gordon in the eye. And I found Cecily's morbid curiosity disturbing. The Campbells were supposed to have been her friends. Had she no pity?

"I'd like you to meet my friend, Nick Yost." I introduced the couple as Nick stood up. "Why don't we all go somewhere and sit down and have a beer."

"No can do," Gordon said. "We're meeting someone. And we've already been questioned by 'your friend.'"

Cecily shook hands with Nick in an assertive kind of way. "I'm writing a book on the Campbell murders. I've talked to all our neighbors on Orange Street. I'd like to interview you, Detective Yost. You too, Ashley."

"I'm really tied up with the case right now, Mrs. Cushman. Maybe later, when things settle down."

Gordon leered knowingly. "Yes, I can see how tied up you are."

How dare he? After what I'd overheard. "What about you, Gordon? Anyone you're 'tied up' with?"

He glared at me. "You used to be a nice little girl, Ashley. But living in New York has robbed you of your Southern charm. Now you're as brash as any Yankee." Gordon turned on his heel.

"What was that all about?" Nick asked.

"Tell you later."

It wasn't hard to understand why Gordon was attracted to Mirabelle. Mirabelle was full of energy, earthy. Cecily was aggressive and intense. She looked like a passionate embrace would snap her in two. So why wouldn't Gordon prefer lusty Mirabelle? Yet I'd overheard him say he loved Cecily, that he didn't want to hurt her. Actually, he'd said he didn't want her hurt again. I wondered what he'd done to hurt her the first time.

"Your turn," Nick said, holding the director's chair for me. "Thanks for trying to help. Since Mr. Cushman is such a busy man, think I'll invite him down to the station. That'll get his attention. Warner too."

Later, with our drawings rolled up in plastic carrier bags, we continued our stroll, stopping at arts and crafts booths and to watch a shag contest.

Nick caught my hand and turned me to face him. "You've got a glow. I knew this would be good for you."

Later, we slowly trudged up the hill to Campbell House where we'd left our cars. I decided to wait for another time to tell Nick about Gordon and Mirabelle's affair. Why spoil our lovely afternoon with talk of their sordid affair?

Mirabelle's Mercedes was parked at the curb. "She's still here. I'd better go in and help her lock up the cutlery."

"Do you have to? I've got the night off and I was hoping we could spend it together."

"I wish I could. But I'd better get in there. She was really angry that equipment was left out. Another time?"

"How about tomorrow? Want to do something?"

"Yes, I'd like that. If it's nice, I'll borrow Melanie's boat and we can take a run down the waterway."

"Sounds great." He brushed a curl off my forehead.

On impulse, I kissed him on the cheek. "Thanks for a lovely afternoon, Nick."

He traced the length of my jaw with his fingertips, then lifted my chin and kissed me fully on the lips. A magic kiss, full of promise. This can't be happening to me, I thought as my knees turned to jelly.

"See you tomorrow," he said, smiling into my face.

His voice and expression had a soft quality I hadn't seen before. I pushed through the gate and started up the walk. I turned and waved as he drove off.

The front door was closed but not locked. I stepped into the silent house. Glancing at my watch, I saw it was seven. In another thirty minutes, darkness would set in. Willie's crew must have gone home for supper. Tomorrow was Sunday and no work would be done on a Sunday.

"Mirabelle? You here?" I called.

My soft-soled sneakers didn't make a sound as I crossed the great hall to check the dining room where I'd last seen Mirabelle unpacking boxes. Everything looked the same. But no Mirabelle.

"Mirabelle!"

The rosy glow of a fine sunset shone dimly through the windows. Deep shadows filled the corners. Boxes were open, their lids folded back. Excelsior and foam peanuts littered the floor. A brown boot jutted out from behind a crate. My breath caught in my throat. I leaned over the crate.

Mirabelle lay on the floor, facedown. The polished wood handle of her German-made carbon steel chef's knife protruded from between her shoulder blades.

TWENTY-ONE

I RAN TO HER SIDE, wanting to help. Every instinct told me not to move her for fear I'd cause her to bleed even more than she had. But then I saw that she'd stopped bleeding and the blood around the wound was drying. I knew what that meant: her heart wasn't pumping. I dashed out to my car, grabbed my purse from under the front seat, and plunged back into the darkening house. I looked at Mirabelle again to verify that my eyes hadn't played tricks on me.

She hadn't moved. The knife handle protruded between her shoulder blades. Nick couldn't be more than a few blocks away. I pulled out my cell phone and punched in his number. The phone rang twice. "Pick up, pick up!"

At his crisp "Yost," I cried, "Nick, come back! Mirabelle's been stabbed! I think she's dead."

"I'll be right there! Get out of that house! Now, Ashley! Wait for me outside."

I gave Mirabelle one final glance. No one could be that still and not be dead. The house seemed watchful, as if eyes peered from every dark corner. The murderer could be here, hiding behind a row of crates, or inside one of the corner cupboards.

I ran for the open door, kicking something across the

floor that landed with a ping. A key. I picked it up and dropped it in my purse. Then I made tracks.

In the few minutes I'd been inside, the sun had gone down and dusk was closing in. I waited nervously on the sidewalk, hugging myself and hopping from one foot to the other, trying to warm up. I felt so cold and shaky. Hurry, Nick, hurry! A blue-and-white Wilmington P.D. cruiser, siren screeching, skidded to a stop in a pile of leaves. Two uniformed officers got out and trotted up to me.

"You Miss Wilkes?" one asked.

"Yes."

"We're supposed to meet Detective Yost here. You found a body?"

"She's inside. I think she's dead. Somebody stabbed her!"

"We'll check it out. Got an ambulance on the way."

"Do you want me to show you where she is?"

"No, ma'am, you stay right here. Just give us a general idea."

"Dining room, behind some boxes. On your right through the hall. You can't miss it." They started off. "I mean you can't miss the dining room," I called after them. The dining room, not the body.

When I turned around, Nick was jumping out of his car. A second cruiser roared up behind it.

Nick paused long enough to touch my arm. "You OK?"

"I think so. Oh, Nick, it was awful. Someone stabbed her."

He took me by the shoulders. "Ashley, sit down, here

in the grass. Put your head between your knees. I'll be right out. Don't leave, Ashley. Do you hear me?"

"Yes, Nick. I'll wait."

He called to the second set of officers. "Cover the back."

Already the neighbors were coming out of their houses. The other two officers followed Nick into the house.

I dropped onto the grass, hugging my purse to my chest. Up and down Orange Street people were gawking. A crowd gathered on the sidewalk. Hadn't there been enough excitement at Campbell House, they were probably asking each other.

A couple in red baseball caps hurried around the corner and pushed their way to me. Someone sat down beside me. "Ashley, what's going on?" Muffie Warner asked breathlessly.

I looked into her face. It was hard to focus. "Muffie?"

"We're here, Ashley. Sherm and me. We live next door, remember? You OK? Someone said there's been another murder." Her face glistened with greedy excitement.

I looked up. Sherman was watching me carefully. He carried Muffie's camera. "We were out taking pictures," he explained.

My voice trembled. "Oh, Muffie, Mirabelle's been stabbed. I think she's dead."

"And you found her?"

"Yes. It was awful. She's been murdered, too."

"Did you...did you see anything? The murderer?" She took her camera from Sherman and focused it on the door to the house where police were wandering in and out. But it's too dark for a good photograph, I thought foolishly.

"There you are!" a woman cried shrilly.

I looked up. Street lights had come on, still it was difficult to see.

Melanie's blurry face leaned over me. "I've been looking all over for you. And calling you for hours." Her voice echoed as if we were in a tunnel.

I tried to explain that I'd had my purse and cell phone locked in my car all afternoon but the effort was just too great. Jon's face appeared over Melanie's shoulder.

"Why are the police here?" Melanie demanded. "If we hadn't come in a police car ourselves, we'd never have gotten through."

"A police car?" My head was spinning. Everything seemed to fade in and out. A drone like mad hornets filled my ears. Curious faces stared at me across the fence. More police cars arrived. An ambulance. Even a fire truck. Muffie was snapping pictures furiously.

Mirabelle was dead. I was sure of it now. If she were alive, they'd be running with her on a stretcher, rushing her to the hospital. But they weren't. So she *was* dead. No need to hurry.

Melanie grabbed me by the arm and tried to drag me to my feet. "Where were you? I've been looking for you. Come on. Get up."

"Melanie, stop. I have to wait for Nick."

Jon grabbed Melanie's wrist and pulled her away. "Leave her alone! Can't you see she's in shock."

"She found Mirabelle," Muffie said.

Jon asked tenderly, "What happened, Ashley?"

"Mirabelle's been murdered. I found her body." A

sharp pain, like a knife, stabbed my chest. This is what Mirabelle had felt when she was knifed in the back. Did she know her killer? Had he stabbed her in the back because he knew her and didn't have the courage to face her? Or maybe he'd sneaked up behind her while she was bent over a box, grabbed the knife and…I fanned my face with my hand.

"She doesn't know how it happened," Muffie said.

"Dear God, not another murder," Jon groaned.

Melanie was all over me. "Oh, baby sister, I'm so sorry. But we've been trying to find you. Mama's missing. Those idiots at Magnolia Manor lost her. The police are looking for her. One of the cops down at River-fest thought he saw her. You've got to help us find her."

"I'm coming," I said.

TWENTY-TWO

"HOW DID MAMA GET all the way from Magnolia Manor to Riverfest?" I asked.

"How in the world do I know," Melanie replied crossly.

"Maybe she hid in the back of a visitor's car," Jon suggested.

"Now there's a happy thought," I grumbled.

We were squeezed in the back of the squad car with Sherman and Muffie, who had insisted on coming along. In the front seat, separated from us by an iron grill, two police officers chatted casually together while the static-laced voice of the dispatcher floated in and out. The car covered the few blocks to the riverfront in what seemed like a matter of seconds and the seven of us spilled out like clowns out of a Volkswagen Beetle.

One of the cops took charge. "OK folks, listen up. I'm handing out cards with my cell phone number on it. Now, we'll split up and search for her. Call if you find her. Otherwise, we'll meet back here at the car in thirty minutes."

We fanned out in different directions: Sherman and Muffie going together, Jon, Melanie, and I going separately.

I retraced my steps along the promenade where earlier Nick and I had our caricatures sketched. The tone of the festival had altered with the coming of nightfall. The children were gone and with them the family atmosphere. Funky Eighties and Nineties music played. Bob King was sitting on the edge of the stage, watching the crowd.

Sara Beth Franks's paintings were still propped against the promenade wall. I spotted Gordon and Cecily Cushman selecting a canvas and buying it. I gave the three of them a shaky wave and asked if they'd seen my mother. I got some pretty weird looks, but the three said no, they hadn't seen her.

Anxiously, I scanned each face in the crowd. Oh, Mama, where are you? What have you done?

A rowdy mob milled around Riverfront Park in front of the Federal Building. I couldn't break through. Most were men about forty with long greasy hair and Grateful Dead T-shirts. Their girlfriends had hard faces and wore short shorts that showed off a lot of tan leg.

I felt a tug as my purse was ripped off my shoulder. With a firm grip on my end of the strap, I tried to turn around to confront the purse snatcher but the crush of bodies hemmed me in. Looping the strap around my wrist, I gave it a good yank. Whoever had hold of the other end, let go, then chopped me on the back of my neck. I was knocked forward into one of the Deadheaders, plowing into his back.

"Hey, man!" he growled, whirling and glaring at me. Quickly, he took in the situation. "You OK? Hey, guys, help this girl."

I was supported by them, buoyed up. Hands reached out to steady me, to lift me to my feet. I looked into their faces. Had one of these guys hit me? It didn't seem possible, they were too eager to help. I still had the purse. The strap was ripped off at one end!

"Thanks," I said, rubbing my neck. "I think I'm OK. Must've tripped."

"No sweat," the guy said.

The girls formed a tight knot around me. Their hard eyes flicked over me, sizing me up. Whatever they saw, they decided I wasn't after their men and backed off.

I tucked the purse under my arm, squeezing it into my side. "Thanks again," I called, taking a step backward. The ring broke up, the Deadheaders and their charming ladies moved away, and I was forgotten. Eagerly, I scanned the crowd, trying to see who'd struck me. I didn't see a familiar face.

The noise was deafening with loud voices vying with high-volume music. I felt small and vulnerable. I just wanted to find my mother and get out of there, flee to the safety of my home, and sort out everything that had happened today. I made my way down Water Street as far as the Cotton Exchange parking lot.

There, pressed against a piling for support, was my mother. She looked overwhelmed, scared out of her wits. "Mama," I cried and wrapped my arms around her.

"Ashley," she sighed. "You found me. Take me home. I just want to go home."

So do I, Mama, I wanted to say.

HOURS LATER, I GOT my wish. I was safely inside my own home. I double-locked the front door behind me and checked the back door and windows. Then I closed all the plantation shutters. I knew what I knew. Someone had attacked me. Someone had tried to steal my purse. But who? And why?

Poor Mama, she'd been so confused. She seemed to have no idea how she'd gotten to the riverfront. She turned to stone when the police questioned her. Melanie and I and the police officers returned her to Magnolia Manor. The look on her face when we said goodnight had broken my heart. Melanie was very upset. So was I. We all were. What a terrible day in the life of the Wilkes family!

Who had stabbed Mirabelle? All the people with a possible motive had been in the area at the time of the murder. I ticked off the suspects. Gordon Cushman, Mirabelle's lover, who wanted his money back and whom she'd threatened with blackmail had been at Riverfest. And Water Street was less than a ten minute walk to Campbell House.

Bob King had been at Riverfest too. I'd seen him working with the sound technicians. And King hated Mirabelle and had vowed to get even with her for taking work from his union.

Sara Beth Franks had been there too, offering her paintings for sale on the promenade. Was there a relationship between Sara Beth and Mirabelle? I wondered what Nick had learned about her.

Sherman and Muffie Warner had been walking toward Campbell House when Nick and I met them. They lived next door but after I found Mirabelle, they had come from the alley behind Campbell House.

Sherman had said they were out taking pictures. In the dark? But what motive would the Warners have to murder Mirabelle? Was Sherman an investor in one of Mirabelle's product line schemes? Had she persuaded Sherman to raise venture capital for one of her enterprises, and then something went wrong? Mirabelle had her fingers in more than fruit pies, that was for sure.

Nick should question all of them, have them account for their whereabouts from five to seven. In my book, they were all suspects.

I got undressed and stepped into a warm, soothing shower. Slipping into a comfortable pink cotton knit pants outfit, I poured a glass of wine.

I jumped at the knock on my door. Flipping on the porch light, I looked through the sidelight. Nick was on my front porch, pacing back and forth.

"Just a sec," I called, and raced into the bathroom to fluff up my hair and apply pink lip gloss.

"Hi," I said softly, holding the door for him.

Pushing past me, he said angrily, "I told you to wait."

"Melanie came and got me," I explained. "With the police. Mama was missing from Magnolia Manor, and we had to find her. Didn't the other officers tell you?"

"No!"

Well, that took the wind out of his sails. He softened. His anger was all about his concern for me. "I was worried about you." He reached out his arms and pulled me close. "There's a murderer out there. It scares me that you might have been in that house with him. Ashley, I couldn't stand it if anything happened to you."

I had no backbone when it came to Nick.

He held me out from him so he could look into my face. "Did you find your mother? Is she OK?"

"We found her at Riverfest, then drove her back to Magnolia Manor and waited while the nurse put her to bed. They gave her a sleeping pill. Guess she'll be on some kind of medication from now on."

He gazed at me thoughtfully. "Yeah," he sighed, "she probably will."

He led me to a one of the love seats, his glance taking in the room. "We've got to talk."

This was the first time he'd been inside my home, and I hated that it wasn't a normal date but related to a murder investigation.

"What's wrong?" I asked, seeing how he was bracing himself. I thought I might laugh, inappropriate as such a reaction might be. "I mean in addition to Mirabelle's being murdered, and my mother being missing, and me being without a job. I'm on the verge of hysteria here," I confessed, "and your attitude is not helping."

He put one arm around my shoulder and lifted my chin with his free hand. "I'm here for you, Ashley. And you're strong. You'll make it through this. Now listen to me. I want you to promise me you won't go back in that house."

"I guess you've got it sealed again." I groaned. "Why would I go back? The woman I was restoring it for is dead. There's no reason for me to go back."

"I'm sorry about that. I know you'd have done a

wonderful job. But there's danger there, Ashley. When I think of you walking into that house alone when a killer could have been hiding in a closet or another room…. Well, just don't do it again, not for any reason."

"I already said I won't." Oh, how I wished he wasn't a cop. His profession was already creating problems for us and we'd barely begun to build a relationship.

"There are things I have to tell you," I said, thinking of the conversation I'd overheard last night between Gordon Cushman and Mirabelle.

"There's something I have to tell you too," he said, pulling away but taking both my hands in his. "I have to tell you this myself because you're going to find out, and I don't want you thinking I'm going behind your back."

"You're scaring me, Nick. What is it?"

His voice softened as if to lessen the impact of his words. "We have to bring Melanie in for questioning about Mirabelle's murder."

"What?"

"Someone saw her entering the house alone shortly after 6:00 p.m. And we've learned that Mirabelle was about to make a lot of trouble for Melanie over the sale of the house. Ethics violations and misrepresentation of its value, according to Mirabelle's lawyers."

He pulled an envelope out of his jacket pocket. "This was in Ms. Morgan's car. Technically, I shouldn't be showing it to you, but I want you to read it."

The letter was addressed to Mirabelle and detailed how her lawyers, acting on her instructions, had drawn

up a lawsuit against Melanie Wilkes that sought resti-
tution and damages in the matter of Ms. Wilkes's professional misconduct. Ms. Wilkes, it went on to say, had
misrepresented the value of Campbell House when she
sold it to Ms. Morgan. The papers were at the law offices
and would be filed with the Clerk of Court at the New
Hanover County Courthouse, just as soon as Ms. Morgan came in to sign them.

"She was threatening to have the state pull Melanie's
license," he said softly.

"But, Nick, the only reason Melanie went into the
house was to find me. She admits that she was there
looking for me. My car was parked out front; it was
logical for her to think I was inside. She told me she
walked around and didn't see anyone, then figured I was
at Riverfest, which was correct. You couldn't see
Mirabelle's body unless you looked behind the crates."

"She'll have a chance to defend herself, Ashley. Tell
her to get a good criminal lawyer." Nick was trying to
reassure me, but ended up frightening me even more.
"Now what did you want to tell me?"

I repeated the conversation I'd overheard between
Gordon and Mirabelle and how she'd threatened to
blackmail him. It was all I could do to keep my mind
on what I was saying. I kept thinking that Melanie was
in danger of being arrested for murder. No, I wouldn't
let that happen. She was the only immediate family I
had. Besides, she was innocent. Melanie couldn't
commit murder any more than I could.

"I'll check Cushman's alibi," Nick said. "This is by

TWENTY-THREE

I SAT BOLT UPRIGHT out of a sound sleep. The brass key I'd kicked then picked up went to Campbell House's front door! I could hardly wait for daylight so I could test my theory.

Seven o'clock on a Sunday morning is the most peaceful time of the week downtown, and I was sure I wouldn't encounter anyone when I returned to the scene of the crime—forgive me, Nick. I dressed in narrow-legged jeans, flats, and a navy turtle neck. I gave my curls a few licks with a brush and slipped silver hoops through my ear lobes. Then I ran out of my house.

Again, the sky was clear, the morning sun evaporating a thin blanket of dew. Next door, my mother's empty house was a silent reminder of just how much our lives had changed. I planned to visit Mama that afternoon, and although I was determined to return home in time to change clothes for church, here I was about to add another sin to my list of confessions.

On Orange Street, bright yellow crime scene tape was strung along the wrought iron fence like a festive garland. I drove past the house, turned at the corner, and parked behind a tall oleander bush in the narrow service alley that ran behind the mansion. Proceeding the rest of the way on foot, I moved stealthily around a construction Dumpster, through high, damp grass under tall trees. I skirted the side of the house, and came around to the portico. Crime scene tape formed a large X over the door. I pulled it loose. The door was large and thick. The lock was vintage brass with ornate carvings that desperately needed a polishing. Not my responsibility anymore, I reminded myself sternly.

I withdrew the brass key from my jeans pocket and inserted it into the lock. It slid in smoothly. Giving it a turn, I felt the bolt snap into the casing. I was locking the door, for without the key, we'd never been able to secure the lock after the locksmith had opened it.

Next I turned the key in the opposite direction and tripped the cylinder. Now it was unlocked again and I removed the key and tucked it inside my jeans pocket.

Taking an ordinary chrome-plated key out of my other pocket, I undid the construction lock. The door swung inward smoothly on solid hinges without a creak. Since I'd come this far, I might as well go all the way. I glanced over my shoulder. Not a sign of life on the street. Mrs. Burns's white clapboard cottage showed a blank face. I slipped inside the eerily silent house, moved through the great hall and into the dining room on tiptoe.

Everything was as it had been last evening except that Mirabelle's body was gone. Where she had lain, a dark rusty stain spread over the floor. Blood had seeped into the old wood.

I wandered out to the staircase and sank down on the bottom step. If Mirabelle had the original key to

Campbell House, why hadn't she told us? She knew we were looking for it.

But wait a minute, I was assuming that the key had been dropped by Mirabelle. Perhaps the killer had dropped it in his—or her—haste to escape.

I sat on the cold steps holding my head in my hands. My brain spun with ideas, making me dizzy. "OK," I said out loud, enlisting the house in my thought processes, "let's review what we know and what we don't know. I found a key on the floor near Mirabelle's body. The key fits the front door. It might have fallen from Mirabelle's purse, or it might have been dropped by the killer.

"If it does belong to the killer, he's probably looking for it now. Is that why he tried to steal my purse last night? How could he possibly know I had the key? Had he been hiding in here, watching me as I discovered the body, seeing when I picked the key up off the floor, saw me put it into my purse?"

There had been a large crowd on Orange Street last night. Of course! The killer had sneaked out by the back door, circled around and stood in the street watching with all the other curiosity-seekers. I considered this new scenario.

Say I'm the killer. I kill Mirabelle. I need that key. I can't find it in Mirabelle's purse because it bounced a distance away when the purse fell, and for some reason I can't stay to look for it. Why? Because Ashley Wilkes is coming up the front walk, and I've got to escape through the back door.

Next, I outlined a second scenario. I'm the killer and

I've got the key but I drop it or it falls through a hole in my pocket. I look for it, but I don't have time to find it because someone, maybe Ashley Wilkes, or maybe even Melanie Wilkes, is coming, and I've got to duck inside a closet.

And why is the key so important? Because it unlocks the Campbells' front door, and the last time that key was used was on the night the Campbells were murdered.

I jumped up and shouted out loud, "So whoever killed Mirabelle killed the Campbells too!"

Nick had made me promise not to come here alone. He thought it was dangerous. Was I in danger? I looked around. Somehow I couldn't picture a murderer attacking me at eight o'clock on Sunday morning with church bells ringing all over town. Whoever killed Mirabelle last evening and whoever attacked me last night would be laying-low, recharging his batteries. Planning his— or her—next evil deed. So, I reasoned, I had a little time to do some detective work of my own.

I climbed the stairs to the second floor and peeked into the room on the left, the oval ballroom with the built-in pipe organ. This is where the dumbwaiter used to terminate. The ballroom looked very much as it had on the night of Reggie and Shelby Campbell's last Christmas party over six years ago. There'd been a Christmas tree and decorations then, and a houseful of guests. Everyone who'd ever been invited to one of the Campbells' parties knew about that dumbwaiter, had probably seen it in use.

Memories of Reggie and Shelby were returning. Reggie had been dashing in a tuxedo, so nice to me, a flustered seventeen-year-old high-school senior at my first formal ball.

I moved down the broad landing to my right and entered the master suite. A large bedroom—Shelby's—with a smaller sleeping chamber nearby where Reggie slept when he'd been out carousing and came in late. Now how did I know that?

I visualized the party again. There was Shelby in her shimmering blue gown, showing off her bedroom to a group of ladies who were depositing their coats on the bed. That was when Shelby had taken a snipe at Reggie, complaining about the late hours he kept.

I toured the suite. There were twin dressing rooms and twin bathrooms. Not much had been removed.

I inspected the bedroom. Inexplicably, this suite had been spared the ravages of time and small critter destruction. With the exception of a thick layer of dust, the suite was very much as it had been when I'd last seen it. The bed was large and dominated the main wall. Elevated on a kind of platform, it was covered with a luxurious satin spread.

From out of nowhere, I experienced another flash of memory. Late the night of the Christmas party, when I'd come back to this room to retrieve Mama's coat, Shelby and another person had been standing together in one of the windows. They'd been whispering, and something about their intimacy had embarrassed me. And they had been embarrassed when I interrupted them, and had jumped apart guiltily. But who was that other person? I couldn't remember a face, only that I'd witnessed something I shouldn't have seen. And I couldn't remember if the person with Shelby had been a man or a woman.

The police had been up here, for some of what I thought was dust was actually a layer of the powder they use to dust for fingerprints.

I glanced at my watch. Time to leave if I was going to return home and dress for church. A hole in the painted woodwork caught my eye as I started toward the door. A fresh gouge, about shoulder height. I stepped close and inserted a fingertip into the hole. Pale inner wood glowed like ivory against the contrasting mahogany frame. Someone had inserted a knife and pried something out. A bullet? I'd never noticed a bullet lodged in this door frame in all the times Jon and I and the crews had swarmed over the house, snapping pictures, taking measurements. But then I'd never been looking for a bullet, had I? Yet it was just the sort of thing the police would look for. And had found.

I moved into the center of the room. Someone had stood in approximately this spot and fired at someone else who'd been fleeing through that door. I lifted my right arm, leveled it, and pulled an imaginary trigger.

TWENTY-FOUR

A CRASH, LIKE THUNDER, reverberated through the house. My hand flew to my heart. What on earth? It was loud enough to raise the dead. A second crash followed, and I recognized the booming chords of the organ. Oh, my God! The ghost! The house was haunted! Old Mrs. Campbell had returned from the dead to play her organ.

I tiptoed out of the master wing, although stealth was certainly not necessary, for whomever or whatever was banging the organ could not hear my footsteps with all the racket being made. And would a ghost care?

Get a grip on yourself, Ashley, I chided myself. Mrs. Campbell had been an accomplished organist. This person plays like a child having a temper tantrum.

A woman stood with her back to me, hunched over the organ's keyboard, randomly striking chords. The ceiling-high pipes vibrated with the sound.

I recognized the back of the woman's head, the cascades of bright orange hair. Only one person I knew had hair like that, and it was not Reggie's mother. "Sara Beth? You almost gave me a heart attack. What are you doing here?"

Sara Beth Franks whirled around. "I might ask you the same thing, Ashley Wilkes," she retorted haughtily.

"I…I left some personal items here. The police said I could pick them up."

"Well, you left the door standing wide open." Sara Beth glided away from the organ and moved around the room, brushing the furniture with her fingertips and leaving trails in the dust. The mirror reflected her progress, two flaming redheads.

Sara Beth always did look like a gypsy. Abundant, bright wavy hair was bound at the nape of her neck in a scrunchie then spilled over her shoulders. She designed and made her own clothes I'd been told, a cross between a peasant and a Bohemian. Her skirt was made of a crinkly orange fabric, cut in triangular shapes so that the hemline dipped into points. An almost shapeless jacket in olive-green covered her plump bosom. Her arms and hands were strong and unusually long for her body, and she wore at least a dozen rings on her fingers.

As I drew nearer, I saw that her topaz chandelier earrings were almost a true match for her eyes. Her white skin seemed incandescent, as if candles burned within, and it stretched tautly over her sharp features.

Sara Beth was driven by some deep, inner resentment. I had never heard her say a kind word about anyone. But she was immensely talented, and her oil portraits and watercolors of coastal scenes hung on the walls of Wilmington's most fashionable living rooms.

Melanie and Sara Beth had gone to high school together. They had been eight years ahead of me in school, and for a grade-schooler that was light-years.

"I have every right to be here," Sara Beth said.

There was something troubling about Sara Beth—scary even. I was beginning to wonder how smart it was to be alone with her.

She waved a white hand in the air. "This should have been my home. I should have been the one to live here with Reggie, not Shelby." She lifted her chin and shot me a challenging look, as if she dared me to disagree. "Reggie was in love with me, you know. Never her."

Tell me more, I wanted to say. "Then his murder must be really rough for you."

She continued to mope about the room as if she were in a trance. "My heart broke when I thought he'd left town without me. If I had known the truth, that he was actually dead, I think I might have killed myself too. Now, well…

"I followed him to Europe, you know, or at least I thought I was following them, that first Christmas when they were supposed to be in Paris. I know Paris well. But I never found them, even though I checked the better hotels. Now we know why. Poor Reggie had never left this house."

She lowered her gaze to the floor as if she could see through it and into the rooms and walls below.

Behind her, tall windows overlooked the tangled garden. The skies had grown quite dark. Funny, only an hour ago, the sun had been shining brightly. Now the sky looked stormy.

"Were you and Reggie lovers when he died?"

"Of course, we were lovers," she cried. "We'd been

lovers since we were sixteen. No one could separate us. I was the love of his life, before he met that awful Mirabelle. No one's happier than I am that she's dead." She stopped at the organ and thumped the keyboard soundly, punctuating her declaration.

"Mirabelle? Reggie and Mirabelle? But she was at least ten years older than he."

Sara Beth regarded me with a contemptuous glare. She ducked her head. She and her reflection continued their ghostly tour around the ballroom. "Oh, Ashley, you are so naive. For a young man of twenty-two, a beautiful woman in her thirties is irresistible. She was gorgeous then, even I have to admit that. And she knew things. Reggie was smitten. He was obsessed with her."

I scarcely breathed. I dared not move for fear I'd break the spell. "Then what happened?" Why hadn't Melanie told me any of this? She must have known.

Sara Beth stopped pacing abruptly and threw herself on the organ bench. "Mirabelle broke his heart, that's what she did. My poor Reggie! She married someone else, and my darling Reggie married Shelby on the rebound."

I took a step toward Sara Beth, cautiously, not wanting to distract her. "Then why didn't he marry you?" I asked softly.

She pulled a handkerchief out of her purse and began to cry into it. "He should have married me."

I moved closer and placed a hand on her shoulder, expecting her to shake it off. When she didn't, I sat down next to her.

She was talking freely now. "I was his true love,

Ashley. I was good for him. Just think, if he had married me, he'd be alive today." She lifted her eyes to mine. There was so much pain in them, I felt sorry for her.

I patted her shoulder. "That might be true."

"I know it's true. It's all my fault. I ran away to Paris so that I wouldn't have to see him and Mirabelle together. Then when Mirabelle broke his heart and Reggie needed me, I wasn't here. So he turned to Shelby. She was always hanging around, just waiting to get her claws into him."

"I'm sorry, Sara Beth." My mind quickly analyzed this news. "But who did Mirabelle marry?"

Sara Beth gave me a withering look. "Don't you know anything? She married Joel Fox. Your sister's new boyfriend."

TWENTY-FIVE

"YOU'VE GOT TO tell me the truth, Melanie."

"Don't I always?" she asked sweetly.

I had located my sister at her real estate office in a faux cottage in a shopping center off Shipyard Boulevard. The front windows of the cottage were filled with placards displaying photographs of houses for sale. The parking slips that fronted a neat white picket fence were empty except for Melanie's boxy Lexus SUV.

"You aren't taking this seriously," I said. "You don't seem to realize how much trouble you're in."

Melanie waved a hand dismissively. "Pish-posh, the police have nothing on me. How could they? I haven't done anything wrong."

"But Mirabelle's lawyers think you did something wrong. That you inflated the price of the house and provided Mirabelle with grounds for a law suit. That you didn't see anything wrong with doubling, or—what?— maybe even tripling the price of a house when as a Realtor you knew its true market value. And when as the owner you were acting as your own agent. Melanie, you could lose your license!"

She rolled her big green eyes heavenward. "That'll

never happen. Why would they sue now? Mirabelle is dead."

"But the police think it's a motive. Nick says someone saw you go into Campbell House at about the time Mirabelle was murdered. The way the police see it you had motive and opportunity. This is serious, Melanie, and if you're not afraid for yourself, I'm afraid for you!"

"I called Walter Brice last night ..."

"Good! Daddy always said he's the best defense lawyer in Wilmington."

"...because those detectives wanted me to go downtown with them. Walt said, and I quote, 'No way. I'm not available now and she can't talk to you without me present. I'll have her in your office on Monday morning and she can answer your questions then. Unless you want to charge her with a crime now.' End of quote. He was wonderful! Older, powerful men are such a turn-on, don't you think?"

"You're crazy if you don't see how much trouble you're in," I said.

Melanie got up from her desk, picked up a potted geranium and left the room. What's wrong with her? I wondered. I followed her into a galley kitchen with a single window at the narrow end. She stood at the sink, outlined by the greenish light from the window.

"Hurricane sky," I murmured.

She shrugged. "Can't get excited about that. We're always having hurricane warnings."

Even on a Sunday morning, catching up on paperwork alone in her office, she had taken pains with her appearance. Her auburn hair was shiny and freshly shampooed. She had on pencil-slim pants and a gold silk sweater set.

Lowering the geranium into the stainless steel sink, she turned the faucet on full blast. The water sputtered, then gushed. Melanie jumped back with a start as a spray of muddy water from the plant splashed her clothing. Grabbing a roll of paper towels, she made ineffectual swipes at her sweater.

"Now see what you've made me do," she wailed.

"I made you do?"

"Well, you've upset me with all your suspicions and talking like I'm about to be carted off to the electric chair."

She burst into tears. My sister never cries, not over anything.

I turned off the water. "Here, give me that." I took the wad of paper towels out of her hand. Gently, I blotted the few wet spots on her cardigan. "It's fine," I said. I handed her a clean paper towel. "Dry your eyes."

"It's not fine," she argued, examining her sweater. "Water stains silk."

"Well, just tell the dry cleaners that it's water and they'll remove the spots. Come on back to your office, we need to talk." I led my sister past empty cubicles and into her own private corner office with its pale blonde furniture and bookshelves, teal carpeting, and original seascapes of Wrightsville Beach painted and signed by Sara Beth Franks.

"She's very talented."

Melanie glanced at the paintings. "They're good. But she's certifiable."

"She is strange, but she's still talented. I met her this morning and she filled me in on a lot I didn't know."

Melanie stopped crying and eyed me warily. "Like what?" she asked suspiciously.

"Well, for one thing, Sara Beth said that Reggie was in love with her and they'd been lovers from the time you all were in high school together until he met Mirabelle, and then Mirabelle seduced him. Is that true?"

"Oh, how would I know?" Melanie replied irritably. "Why is Sara Beth dredging up all this stuff now? It's ancient history. I don't know what Reggie ever saw in her anyway. He was a hunk even then, good-looking and popular, a great sports car, and filthy rich."

She seemed resentful. Was it possible she'd had a crush on Reggie too? "So it's true then."

"Well, they dated, that much is true. But as for Reggie being in love with her, I think she made that up. If he was in love with her, why didn't he marry her? Why did he marry Shelby? I think it's all in her head."

"What happened between him and Mirabelle? Sara Beth said they were lovers."

"I think he had a fling with her. I was at Chapel Hill at the time, you know, and you were still in junior high, but later when I came home from college and started out in the real estate business, it seems to me that Reggie was spending a lot of time in Atlanta with Mirabelle. That's where she lived in the early Nineties."

"And then Mirabelle dropped him to get married. Married to Joel Fox, Melanie," I pointed out dramatically.

"Well, they weren't married for very long! Just long enough for Joel to launch her in television in Atlanta. He worked for Ted Turner, you know. When he realized what she was really like, he divorced her and moved out to Hollywood. It was a smart move for him because he hit it really big time in the movie business."

"And are you two dating?"

Melanie's smile was smugly satisfied. "Of course, we're dating. We've become very close. He's my new sweetie, if you must know. At first, he was just a hot prospect, but now…well, I'm showing him commercial properties in the area, and when we find the right one he's going to develop a resort hotel that will set this little town on its heels. Who knows, this may be the guy who'll get me to settle down." She was practically purring.

I had heard that one before. "I'm just so upset that the police think you had anything to do with Mirabelle's murder."

"That's nonsense. Nick Yost is not much of a detective if that's the best he can do. It's true, I was at Campbell House that evening. I must have got there right after Mirabelle was stabbed." She rubbed her arms. "It gives me the willies to think I almost walked in on a murder. The murderer might have been there, hiding. He could have killed me, too. I opened the door and shouted your name. When you didn't answer, when all I heard was quiet, I assumed you'd walked down to Riverfest, and that's exactly what you had done. That's the only reason I was there." One corner of her mouth lifted in a smirk. "If I ever decide to kill someone, there won't be witnesses or an obvious motive."

She got up and went around to her desk chair. "And as for this trumped up lawsuit, all Mirabelle was after was money. My lawyer was already proposing a settlement to her lawyer, but I refused to go along. 'Let her sue,' I told him. I didn't do anything wrong, and she'd have a hard time proving otherwise. The value of houses in the Historic District has escalated."

"Well, we've got to find a way to convince the police of that. Mel, I think whoever killed Mirabelle also killed Reggie and Shelby."

She narrowed her eyes and leaned across her desk. "What makes you think that?"

"I have my reasons." At this point, I didn't intend to tell anyone, not even Melanie, about the key. I had a plan. I was going to find proof that there were better suspects than Melanie, then I'd present Nick with an irrefutable argument. He'd have to change his mind about Melanie.

"I'd still like to know how the cameo brooch got into Shelby's sofa," I said evenly.

Melanie's face closed up. "I don't want to talk about that brooch. Not now, not ever. Come on. I'm taking you to brunch."

TWENTY-SIX

SUNDAY BRUNCH AT ELIJAH'S is a Wilmington tradition. Originally a maritime museum, the riverfront building had been converted to a restaurant years ago. Melanie knew everyone who counted, so it was no surprise when the manager hustled over to escort us to a choice window table. Outside, fat raindrops pelted the Cape Fear River.

By one o'clock the rain was pounding the coast and looked like it could go on for hours. We kept the Mimosas coming while I devoured a three-egg omelet filled with shredded artichoke hearts and gorgonzola cheese. Between bites, I related the conversation I'd overheard at Thalian Hall between Gordon Cushman and Mirabelle. "She threatened to blackmail him, Mel. That's a good motive for murder."

Melanie scrunched up her eyes, the way she does when she's thinking. "Cecily's the one with the gonads in that family. My money's on her. She's been running around town questioning everyone about their relationship with Reggie and Shelby." She leaned closer and lowered her voice. "But you know what? I wouldn't put murder past her. She's very possessive of Gordon. And why not? He's a darlin' man, and she looks like a white mole, always peering out over those little half glasses."

She did an impersonation of Cecily that was so on-target, I dissolved into a fit of laughter.

Melanie sobered. "All I know, baby sister, is that I didn't do it!"

I covered her hand with my own. "I know you didn't. And I'm going to prove you are innocent if it's the last thing I do. Let's talk about my theory that whoever killed Reggie and Shelby also killed Mirabelle."

"Now there's a thought to curdle your milk. What makes you think so?"

I shrugged. "Why not?"

"Why not, indeed? It's better than your detective's theory. He's so stupid he thinks I did it when he should be hunting for the real killer. Why, we could all be in danger."

"He is not my detective! Anyway, the police are still investigating." Now why was I defending Nick?

Melanie glanced over my shoulder and groaned. "Don't look now."

Why do people always say that, knowing you'll look anyway? I looked. Sherman and Muffie Warner were table-hopping. "Hey, you two!" Muffie called.

"Hi," Melanie and I said flatly. Muffie got under my skin. And Sherman was hiding something.

"The police told us you found your lost mama," Sherman said with a smirk.

"She's sick, Sherman," I said through clenched teeth. "It might be Alzheimer's disease."

Muffie gave Sherman a jab with her elbow. "We're real sorry about your mama, honey bunch. It must be real hard for you."

Sherman sipped from the Bloody Mary in his hand. "What must be real hard is the way you're always tripping over dead bodies. You're a magnet for murder, Ashley Wilkes."

"I wouldn't regret tripping over your dead body, Sherman," I retorted. "But then, you'll probably die in bed. In New York."

Melanie hooted.

Sherman's eyes shot daggers at me, but I returned his glare with a smirk of my own. That'll learn you, I thought. You'll never make fun of my mama again.

Muffie picked up on the undercurrent. "New York? Why New York? What are y'all talkin' about?"

"Nothing, sugah, just chitchat, is all." Melanie covered her mouth with one hand and fanned the air with the other.

Sherman shot me a hostile glare. If looks could kill. Quickly, he switched subjects. "Did you see anything incriminating at the scene?"

"What do you mean by incriminating?"

"Well, did you catch a glimpse of the killers? Did you find something—a clue?"

Melanie sniffed. "What weird questions you're asking my sister. You sound like the police."

Sherman had said "killers," not "killer." And he specifically asked if I'd found evidence.

His face turned as red as the Bloody Mary. He rushed to explain, so hurriedly, he stammered. "It's just that my, my, my cousin is on the P.D., and he says Mirabelle's keys are missing. She drove herself over to Campbell House. Her car was parked out in the street. Yet she didn't have a set of car keys on her or anywhere around her. They didn't even find a purse. And the keys weren't in the car. The police towed it to the impound lot."

I grabbed a roll and got busy buttering it. What had happened to Mirabelle's purse? The brown leather shoulder bag? I'd seen her reach into and withdraw the Swiss Army knife.

"What do you think of this rain?" Muffie asked brightly.

"What's to think?" I asked irritably.

She let out a snort. "You're so weird, Ashley."

"It's Nancy," Sherman explained, "crouched out there off the Bahamas."

"Who's Nancy?"

Muffie shook her head. "Helloooo? Anybody in there? Where y'all been? Hurricane Nancy. She's headed straight for Wilmington."

I turned to stare out the window. So a hurricane was headed our way. I hadn't listened to the news in days because every time I turned it on, some precious newscaster was saying how Ashley Wilkes, a historic preservationist, had a knack for turning up corpses in old houses. What an endorsement!

Sherman was hyper, hopping from one foot to the other, bumping against waiters. Why doesn't he take the hint and leave? But he loved the sound of his own voice. "Isn't it delicious? Nothing much ever happens in this pokey town. Now we've got two society murders and a killer on the loose."

I looked at Melanie. Her green eyes were throwing off sparks.

Sherman's darting gaze came to rest on her. "Someone said the police are interested in you, hon." He arched his brows. "Now that can't possibly be true, can it?"

"Of course it's not true," Melanie snapped. She shoved back her chair and plunked two twenties on the table. "Lovely to see you, Muffie, Sherman. Do forgive us for rushing off, but we've got to go visit our mama."

I jumped up too, thrusting my napkin on the table. Pushing back my chair, I hastily followed Melanie's lead. She was halfway out of the restaurant.

"Give your mama our love," lame Muffie called after us. "Hope she doesn't get lost again."

I caught up with Melanie outside the ladies' room. She yanked me inside and pressed her fingertip to her lips while she checked out the stalls to be sure we were alone. Then she gave me a level, warning stare. "Don't you ever trust that Sherman Warner. If anyone had a good reason to kill Reggie Campbell, it was him. And don't you ever let him get you alone, either, Ashley Wilkes. I think he could be dangerous." Her green eyes snapped.

"Why? What'd he do?" I asked in a whisper.

"About six months before Reggie and Shelby disappeared, there was a scandal at his brokerage house. Sherman was involved in some shady, insider-trading scam. I happen to know because I was dating his manager Scott at the time and you know how men love to gossip when they're trying to impress you. Well, Scott let a few things slip he shouldn't have. The firm covered up Sherman's fraud, but the one person outside the firm who knew about it and who could make trouble for

Sherman was Reggie Campbell. Sherman and Reggie were thick as blood in those days."

Melanie kept her eyes glued to the door. "Scott told me he hoped Sherman and Reggie never had a falling out because Reggie had enough on Sherman to send him to prison for a long, long time."

"So that's what Teddy was referring to," I said.

Melanie started to leave. "Come on." I trailed along behind her. Didn't I always?

The rain had let up. Outside on the boardwalk we bumped into Cecily and Gordon Cushman. "Ashley! How fortuitous! I was going to call you. What are you doing this afternoon? I'm just dying to talk to you, but now's not a good time. I'll call you. My editor is so excited—two murders!—and you made both discoveries. He's so anxious to meet you."

I must have looked blank because she peered inquiringly at me over half-glasses. "You promised to help me with my book."

Gordon was shifting from foot to foot, impatient.

Seeing me hesitate, Melanie interjected, "Excuse us, Cecily, we're on our way to see our mama."

Gordon tried steering Cecily away. Cecily shook off his hand with a sharp, "Bug off, Gordon!"

To me she said, "I'll call you, Ashley. I've told my editor all about you. He's got a lot of influence so you don't want to cross him. He'll get you a free trip to New York and an interview on the *Today* show with me. Why, he might even get us on *Oprah!* Don't you just love it?"

"She's a ghoul," I told Melanie's back. "She had the

TWENTY-SEVEN

MAMA SEEMED HAPPY and relaxed. The tension and fearful attitude was gone. Her doctor was trying a mild tranquilizer and it seemed to help. In the course of two days she'd found herself a suitor, a dapper older gentleman who followed her around the solarium, answering to the name she'd tagged him with, Rhett.

"She's my Scarlett," he confided to Melanie and me. "Your mother's a pistol. Do you think she'll marry me?" He was so earnest I was touched. What a sweet old gent.

After a lengthy visit that included "Rhett," we dashed out into the rain to our separate cars. Melanie had houses to show, so we drove off in different directions. I headed for home.

Jon's car was parked in front of my house and I found him waiting for me in the wicker swing on my front porch. Good, old, reliable Jon. He wasn't making trouble for me and my sister. He doesn't make me feel like I'm on a roller coaster. I was so happy to see him I threw my arms around his neck.

"Hey, what'd I do to deserve that?" he asked, grinning. "Tell me quick. Whatever it is I'll do it again."

"Can't it be as simple as I'm glad to see you? Mama's adjusting so well at the nursing home. She's in her element out there. A regular belle of the ball. And I'm feeling pretty good about it."

"I'm glad to hear this, Ashley. I was hoping you'd show up. Want to go out and get a bite? The rain is letting up."

"Sure, just let me grab a quick shower and change into some fresh clothes."

"I'll wait for you out here. It's peaceful and the rain has cooled things off."

"Well, at least let me bring you a glass of wine."

"I won't refuse that."

"HAVE YOU GOT other jobs lined up?" I asked. I studied his profile as he drove. He had on a casual Rugby shirt with tan slacks. He looked nice, and he smelled good. Now why can't I fall for him, I asked myself, instead of an impossible homicide detective who makes me crazy?

"I've got some jobs lined up, yes, and don't you worry, you'll get something too. I'm watching out for you."

He took the drawbridge across the Intracoastal Waterway, followed the causeway that split Harbour Island down the middle, then crossed Banks Channel on yet a second bridge, touching down on Wrightsville Beach. The Oceanic Restaurant was located at a pier that jutted out into the ocean. By now the rain had let up, but humidity clung to our hair and clothing as we walked from the car. Fog loomed over the ocean. From a distant buoy, a foghorn echoed forlornly. The sea was rough tonight. In the darkness, powerful waves pounded the beach. There would be riptide warnings in the

morning but that wouldn't keep the surfers out. Someone would drown. It happened every fall.

As we scurried up the ramp to the restaurant, Jon
said, "The latest report is that the hurricane will bypass
us. The weather forecasters say it'll skirt Wilmington
and move on to Nags Head. Remember how much damage Fran did? Some of the beach houses she destroyed
will never be rebuilt."

"I feel safer on the mainland with the barrier islands
between me and the storms. But your house is right out
here in the open and surrounded by water. Doesn't that
worry you?"

"Sure, it does. But I've been lucky so far and maybe
my luck will hold. Look at it this way, Ashley, when it's
not storming, I live in paradise."

Looking over the menu, we decided to share the
Captain's Birthday Sampler, a selection of fish and
seafood panfried in butter. I ordered a cup of She Crab
soup to start.

"Tell me what you know about Sherman Warner," I
said. "Melanie and I saw him and Muffie at Elijah's and
she warned me he might be dangerous. And Teddy says
Reggie had something on him."

"Guess they're referring to that old business about
some shady stocks."

"Melanie indicated he was involved in some insider-
trading scheme. Did everyone know about it?" I
wondered if knowledge of Sherman's troubles was
widespread. "I don't remember myself. I was still in
high school and I wouldn't have been interested."

"Thanks a lot for making me feel old." But he grinned. "Not many people knew."

"But you did."

"I heard from a friend at his brokerage house that Sherman pushed some worthless stocks that lost Reggie money. If Reggie had filed a complaint with the S.E.C., at the very least Sherman would have had compliance problems and no one would have hired him. Worst-case scenario, he'd have gone to prison."

"But do you think he'd have killed Reggie over that?"

"To save his own skin? Who knows? I don't know what makes Sherman tick. He's always 'on' when I see him."

"That's the way he comes across to me too. Everything's staged and phony and I wonder if he's on uppers, he's so hyper. So if he did go after Reggie, then Shelby just happened to be in the way, so she had to die too." I flashed back to my scenario of Shelby's fatal fall down the staircase.

"Someone killed them, Ashley," Jon said soberly, "and now Mirabelle's dead too. I've been trying to convince myself that whoever killed Reggie and Shelby was long gone from this town years ago, but with Mirabelle's death, I can't fool myself any longer."

"That's what I've been thinking. The three murders are connected. Whoever killed Mirabelle killed Reggie and Shelby, too. Why doesn't Nick see that?"

"Maybe he does. The police would be keeping their leads quiet."

I hoped that was true.

The waiter brought our order and we divided it. "Jon, who among that crowd traveled to Europe when those phony postcards were mailed back home?"

"As I recall most of that crowd traveled a lot. Sherman and Muffie went often. They said they tried looking up Shelby and Reggie but couldn't find them. And Gordon and Cecily took one of those epicurean tours of France and Italy."

"Italy? Teddy said his mother got a post card from Shelby one summer from Tuscany. So either the Warners or the Cushmans could have sent a fake postcard."

Jon looked thoughtful. "You know, even your mother and Melanie went to Europe that next summer."

"You're right! They stayed overnight with me in New York before flying out of JFK."

TWENTY-EIGHT

"Ms. MORGAN HAS GOT a lot of fans out there and every one of them is ringing the chief's phone off the hook. They're demanding we bring in her killer." Nick stood in the middle of my living room. It was late and we were both tired.

"And so you're going after Melanie who wouldn't harm a fly!"

Hot tears stung my eyes and I covered my face with my hands. The gulf between us grew wider and deeper with every quarrel. Not even the roses he'd brought me, lush and velvety as they were, could bridge the gap. I was determined not to let him see me cry.

I felt him move in, felt his hands cup my elbows. His jacket smelled of rain, and his face, so close to my own, smelled lingeringly of aftershave. I lowered my hands as far as my chin and fixed him with a defiant stare. What I saw in his eyes surprised me. Pain, confusion. His extraordinary hazel eyes, usually scrunched up in a scowl so he wouldn't give away any emotion, brimmed with compassion because I was hurting.

"I know what you're going through," he said softly.

I pulled my arms out of his grasp. "No, you don't! You might understand how it's torn me up to have to institutionalize Mama, but you have no idea what you're putting me through because you're being so pigheaded. You're blind and stubborn. You don't have a sister—an innocent sister—who's being accused of murder by the person who is …" I stopped. Who's what? The man I'm falling in love with?

"Who's supposed to be my friend," I finished lamely, admitting to myself that I didn't know what we meant to each other. I gave myself a shake. This was no time to be evaluating my relationship with Nick. Melanie was in trouble.

"I'm not accusing her of murder, Ashley. But when evidence against her comes in, I can't ignore it."

Again, I noticed how tired he seemed. This hurts him too, I realized. Nervously, I said, "Sit down, Nick. I've got to find a way to convince you that Melanie is not a murderer. I'm going to tell you some things that I haven't…well, I haven't had a chance to tell you before."

He moved around to the opposite side of the coffee table and sat on the white love seat.

"There are many people who have a motive for murdering Mirabelle," I said. Calmly, I related the quarrel I'd witnessed between Mirabelle and Bob King, the labor leader. "King threatened her. He said that some day she was going to get what she deserved. You saw for yourself how irrationally he behaved at the party. The next day Mirabelle was murdered."

Nick did not comment as I went on.

"She humiliated people who worked for her, like me and Jon, and her assistant Teddy Lambston. Then there's the money she owed Gordon Cushman, a half million dollars that she refused to repay because they were having an affair. She threatened she'd tell his wife about the affair if he refused to wait for the money. That's blackmail. Now that Mirabelle is dead, Cushman will be able to collect from her estate."

I related everything I could remember about the conversation I'd overheard between Mirabelle and Gordon. "Don't you see? There were others with strong motives and opportunity. You should be investigating all of them."

Nick leaned forward, elbows on knees, hands clasped. "Ashley, I assure you I am investigating this murder from every angle. Jon told me about the quarrel in Ms. Morgan's office. I looked into it. King has an alibi for the period from five to 7:00 p.m. on Saturday evening when she was murdered."

"Did you check King's alibi? If his union friends are providing the alibi, they're in on it too. They hated Mirabelle as much as he did."

"You're suggesting a conspiracy?"

"Well, why not? A conspiracy by union members, or by Gordon and Cecily Cushman, or by Sherman and Muffie Warner, is as believable as your idea that Melanie did it!"

"Ashley, for the last time, it's not my idea that Melanie did it! I am simply conducting an investigation, and your sister is someone we've got to look at."

I jumped up and paced the length of my living room, then whirled around. "You saw Sherman and Muffie with your own eyes in the area right before Mirabelle was killed."

"But Ashley, they live next door. They had every right to be there."

"And they could have stopped at Campbell House."

"But no one saw them do that. But an eye witness did see Melanie go inside. Plus, what's their motive?" He ran his hand over his hair.

"Here's a motive for you. Sherman Warner was involved in some serious S.E.C. violations several years ago. Pushing bad stocks or insider trading, something like that. It never got as far as an investigation because his manager covered for him, but a few people in town knew about it. Maybe one of them was Mirabelle. Maybe she's been blackmailing him and he got tired of paying."

"But that's just speculation, Ashley."

"There's more, Nick," I argued. "Reggie knew about the S.E.C. violations too, and he was in a position to ruin Sherman's career. So that'd give Sherman a good reason to kill Reggie and Shelby and Mirabelle. I'm convinced that whoever killed the Campbells killed Mirabelle too. Those murders are connected."

"By what, Ashley? Other than they happened in the same house, there's no connection."

"Oh, yes, there is. Wait here a sec." I went into my bedroom and removed the key from the pocket of the jeans I'd worn that morning. I returned to the living room and placed it in Nick's hand.

He looked down at it, then up at me in awe. "The missing key. Where did you find it?"

"On the floor near Mirabelle's body."

"You've had it since yesterday! You should have given it to me. This is evidence in a homicide case."

"I know. In all the excitement I forgot about it. I didn't know what it meant until yesterday when I tried it in the door."

"You went back to that house!"

"Oh, chill out, Yost! You are not the boss of me. Now listen for once in your life. The last time that key was used was the night the Campbells were murdered. The murderers locked up the house and drove away, posing as Reggie and Shelby. You know all that. So, this key has been in the murderer's possession for the past six years until I found it on the floor not far from Mirabelle's body."

I went on, ignoring his stony silence. "Either Mirabelle had it and her killer was trying to take it away from her, or her killer had it and dropped it. Either way, her death is definitely linked to Reggie's and Shelby's murders. Now do you see why Melanie couldn't have done it?"

"What I see is a person I care for withholding critical evidence and repeatedly returning to the crime scene despite my warnings. You're wrong about one thing, Ashley. This is my case, I make the rules, and in this situation I am the boss!"

He shook his head sadly. "I trusted you, Ashley. I didn't think you'd deceive me. Do you have any idea what you've done? If the perp's fingerprints were on this key, you've smudged them by handling it. You say you want to help

Melanie, but you may have just destroyed evidence that could clear her and lead us to someone else."

I hadn't thought of that, yet could I admit it? No way. "I'm not buying into this guilt trip you're laying on me, Nick! I can explain. I was going to give you that key last night. I started to tell you about it when you interrupted me to tell me that my sister was a suspect. Well, let me ask you one thing. If you think the murderer was dumb enough to leave fingerprints, were there prints on the knife handle?"

I could see by his expression that I had him. I wasn't going to let him one-up me; I was as stubborn as he. Yet I also knew in my heart of hearts that the fragile relationship that was developing between us had changed. Without trust, can there be love?

"The knife handle was clean," he said. "Whoever stabbed Mirabelle wore gloves."

"Well then, there wouldn't have been any fingerprints on the key either, would there?"

He was silent for a moment. "Look, Ashley, I care about you, I really do. That creates a conflict for me. I feel like I've got to bend over backward to be impartial, not to let my feelings for you affect my judgment. I wish things were different. I wish the evidence pointed to someone else. But it doesn't."

"Well, look harder," I said, fighting back tears.

"There's more. Now, hold yourself together. I came here to warn you that the case against Melanie has become stronger. You've got to prepare yourself for the possibility that she might have done it."

The blood froze in my veins. "What do you mean?"

"A witness came forward and testified that she overheard Melanie threaten to kill Mirabelle."

"Well, she's just lying," I yelled. "Who said that? Whoever said it is your real murderer. She's trying to set Melanie up."

"It was Muffie Warner. She signed a statement that she overheard a nasty quarrel between Melanie and Mirabelle in the ladies' room at Thalian Hall on Friday night. She claims that Melanie screamed at Ms. Morgan that she'd kill her if she tried to have her real estate license revoked."

I gave him a defiant look. "Oh, Muffie Warner, that lightweight! She's so dumb she doesn't even know her husband is cheating on her."

"Cecily Cushman was there too. But she wouldn't confirm the statement. She said you two have a book deal and she doesn't want to jeopardize that." He looked at me inquiringly.

"We don't have any book deal! Her publisher wants her to interview me for a book she's writing about the murders. I won't do it. I'm trying to build a reputation as a solid professional, someone who is reliable. So I'm not getting involved with one of Cecily's books!"

"Well, deal or no deal, the D.A. can always subpoena her as a hostile witness," Nick said.

"Hostile witness! You've not only accused Melanie, but now you've got her in court on trial. Get out, Nick! Leave right now!"

He moved slowly to the door. "Look, I'm sorry, Ashley, but until this is over, I won't be able see you. Socially, I mean."

TWENTY-NINE

ON MONDAY AFTERNOON, I turned into Summer Rest Road to see emergency vehicles in front of my house. I pulled in behind a police cruiser. Nick's unmarked car was parked directly in front of my house. I've been robbed, I thought.

The CSI mobile unit blocked the street. The door of my house stood wide open. Crime scene technicians and uniformed police rushed in and out. I stepped through my open gate, surprised at how numb I felt.

A police officer stopped me. "You Miss Wilkes?"

I nodded, stumbling on one of the brick pavers. He caught my arm and led me to the porch. Shards of broken glass littered the floor. The sidelight had been punched out.

"This is too much. I can't take any more."

The officer, looking concerned, guided me to the swing. "Why don't you just sit here, ma'am, and try to stay calm. I'll let Detective Yost know you're here."

Detective Yost. Here we go again. Round three, or was it four? Or five? My head was swimming. I leaned back against the cushions and closed my eyes. The swing sank as he joined me. He picked up my hand and held it tight. "Thank God you weren't at home when they broke in." He sounded scared.

"How bad is it?"

"It's a mess. I don't think they found what they were looking for and that's why they tore the place apart. I'm sorry you had to come home to this." He gave my hand a squeeze, then placed it on the swing between us. In a flash he was all business. "Where are the rubies you had on the other night?"

"In a safe deposit box." Seeing his surprised expression, my voice rose somewhere between anger and hysteria. "What's the matter, Nick? Don't you think I have enough sense to keep valuable rubies in a lock box? I just came from the bank."

"Stop fighting me. I'm not the enemy."

"You're not? You could have fooled me."

"Ashley, please…"

"No, Nick. You can't have it both ways. You can't be my friend and go after my sister, then expect I won't mind. I don't trust you. So don't 'Ashley, please' me."

He started to get up. "OK. I've got to get back inside."

"You think they were after the rubies?"

"Your CD system is in there. You'll have to check to see if anything is missing. So yes, I think they were after the rubies."

"Oh, dear lord." I wanted to have a good, hard cry, but I refused to let him see me in tears.

"Brace yourself, Ashley. They tore things up pretty bad."

"How did you get involved?" I asked.

"Your neighbor noticed a suspicious truck cruising the street. Then when he was out walking his dog he saw your door standing open and the sidelight broken. He called 911. He may have scared them off."

I followed him inside. My sweet little house had been violated. I felt violated. Everything was a shambles. Glass shards sparkled on the floor near the door. Nothing had been spared. Every piece of furniture had been ransacked. Drawers and cabinet doors gaped open. Clothing, books, glassware dumped on the floors.

"There's so much anger here," Nick said. "He couldn't find the rubies so he went bonkers."

I rubbed my arms, feeling cold and remote. I wished things were different between Nick and me, so I could burrow into his arms. "This has nothing to do with the rubies," I told him in a wooden tone. "I'm getting close to the murderer."

"Don't start that again, Ashley. Remember, a lot of people saw you wearing those rubies at the party Friday night. Your picture was on the society page in the newspaper on Sunday so anyone could have seen those rubies. And you don't have an alarm system. I want you to get one installed right away. I'll even call it in for you. And get one for your mother's house as well."

A uniformed cop tapped him on the shoulder. "Wait here," he told me as they moved aside and talked softly together.

When he came back, he said, "Look, I've got to go. Your neighbor memorized the license plate of the truck he saw cruising the street. DMV has identified it as Henry Cameron's. He was the Campbells' caretaker. We've got to go talk to him." He started toward the door with the cop, then he seemed to really focus on me. "Don't worry, Ashley. I'll have a cruiser drive by to keep an eye on things. One of the officers will board up that broken window."

After the police left—a sheet of plywood nailed over the broken sidelight as promised—I surveyed my trashed rooms. Where to begin? I followed the cord to my telephone under a pile of books and papers. At least there was a dial tone. I dialed Melanie's cell phone. When she didn't answer, I left a message. She didn't answer at her home number or her office either. I left messages at both places.

I pushed stuff off one of the love seats and settled down heavily. I'd had mixed feelings about Henry Cameron. He had come across as scary with that grim reaper scythe, yet humble too. But why would he break into my house? The key? He wanted the key. Or was Nick right, could he have been after the rubies?

I tried to calm down. Nick would pick him up. Nick would lock him up. Then I'd be safe.

I checked all the locks then tackled the mess.

At four, an ADT van rolled up onto the brick pavers. "You sure got connections," the technician said when I let him in. "Told me this was top priority, to drop whatever I was doing and get out here. Got to do the house next door too."

Two hours later, he showed me how to work the alarms, then left. By that time it was six and I was tired and hungry. I grilled a cheese sandwich and heated milk for hot cocoa. Comfort food. Melanie called. Finally. I told her someone had broken into my house.

"Install a burglar alarm," she advised, after I assured her the burglar had not stolen the family rubies.

"Already taken care of," I said. "Can you come over?"

"Oh, Ashley, I've had a dreadful day. I just want to go home and have a good stiff drink. My lawyer and I met with the police this morning. You'll never believe this but the A.D.A. tried to strike a deal. She had the nerve to ask me to plead to manslaughter? That would never happen if Daddy were alive! I've got a good mind to sue this city!"

"Melanie, did you threaten to kill Mirabelle?"

For a moment she was silent "Who told you that?"

"Nick. Muffie Warner signed a statement. Cecily was there too but for now she isn't saying one way or the other."

"Those two. I ought to kill them."

"Melanie! Did you?"

"Well, yes, but I didn't mean anything by it. It was just something you say in the heat of the moment. No one who knows me would believe I meant it. The bitch brigade is out to get me."

THIRTY

"THEY'RE ALL TALKING about me," Melanie hissed. "I hate them. They're such phonies."

We were at Mirabelle's house for the post-funeral reception.

"It's all that blundering detective's fault. Everyone's shunning me like I'm Lizzie Borden."

Joel slipped an arm around her shoulder. "They're not fit to wipe your shoes on, angel face."

No one shed a tear for Mirabelle. Joel must have felt something for her once—he had been her husband—but if he mourned her now, it was a well-kept secret.

Black-humor jokes made the rounds. Food disappeared faster than Sissy and the other maid could refill the platters. Mirabelle's dining room table was a groaning board, heaped with fried chicken, ham biscuits, cheese biscuits, barbecued ribs: enough cholesterol, growth hormones, antibiotics, and meat tenderizer to send the entire assemblage into cardiac arrest.

"There were no living relatives," someone behind me said. "She left everything to the Historic Preservation Society."

What! Who said that? I whipped around but everyone was talking at once.

"Her one good deed and she had to die to make it happen," another person quipped.

On the other side of the room, Nick was studying the guests. I had resolutely avoided him, yet I couldn't help following the direction of his gaze as he watched Sara Beth Franks deep in conversation with Cecily Cushman. I'd been assuming that the killers were a man and a woman, but could they have been two women? I had only Sara Beth's word for it that she had left town to follow Reggie and Shelby to Paris. Perhaps she was fleeing from murder.

Across the room, Melanie was talking to Teddy. I crossed to join them. Teddy gave me a hug. "I can't believe she's gone. She was such a powerful force, I thought she'd live forever. Who do the police suspect?"

Why did everyone think I had inside info because of my few dates with Nick? "Bob King's at the top of my list." Then I told Teddy about my break-in and all the destruction.

"Poor Ashley. I'll come over and help you clean up if you want."

I looked pointedly at Melanie. Why hadn't she offered to help? "I got a lot of it done last night, but thanks anyway, Teddy."

"I'm going back for seconds. Bring you something? Melanie? Ashley?"

"No, thanks," Melanie said. "I've got to watch my figure."

"Oooh, don't worry. You're a stunner."

"What a sweet guy," she said when he left. "You

know, you're not the only one who's out of work. So is he. You could show a little sympathy."

I blinked. And then, dammit, I felt ashamed.

She went on, "He might be forced to sell his house. He asked me to appraise it for him. I think he'll be surprised at how much it's worth."

Teddy give up his house? "He loves that house, Melanie. What a shame."

Someone touched my arm. "Ashley, a word?"

"Oh, hi, Betty." Melanie moved away to join Joel.

Betty murmured, "Poor Mirabelle didn't have many friends, but her TV audiences loved her. In the end she was more generous than we gave her credit for."

"So it is true."

"Yes, it's true, Ashley. Mirabelle surprised us all. She left us her money, as well as this house and her antiques. We'll sell the house. Best of all, she left us Campbell House."

"What?"

"The Board is in accord. We want you and Jon Campbell to restore Campbell House for us. It was Sheldon Mackie's suggestion. He's such a dear man and he respects your talent. We're going to turn the mansion into a museum and use it as our headquarters. So if you want the job, it's yours."

"Do I! This is the most fantastic news. I can't wait to tell Melanie."

"If you could meet with us soon and submit your plans…it's just a formality."

I kissed her cheek. "Thank you, Betty. You're my fairy godmother."

After that, I could barely keep a straight face. I searched for Nick in the crowd. How much I wanted to tell him. I knew he'd be happy for me.

I wandered to a window, wanting to pinch myself. The sky was milky white, as iridescent as a pearl, so bright it hurt my eyes to look at it. The rain had let up. The meteorologists were having a tough time predicting the storm's path. Nancy was still hundreds of miles out at sea, churning and gathering strength. Where would she strike?

Outside on the front lawn, Gordon Cushman and Sherman Warner were smoking cigars, prancing around each other like bandy roosters. Suspects two and three. Gordon was tall and looked like he worked out. He'd have had no problem disposing of two bodies.

Gordon threw his cigar on the lawn and took a threatening step toward Sherman. He yelled something. Sherman took a step back, put up his fists to defend himself. His lips curled in a snarl.

Gordon lunged at him, fists flying. Then they were grappling with each other and rolling on the ground. Gordon sat astride Sherman's chest, punching the daylights out of him.

"Fight! Fight!" I yelled, pointing outside.

Nick dashed out of the house, followed by several men. "How they love this stuff," Betty said over my shoulder. "Why do men make such a fuss about PMS, when it's testosterone-surge that's the real threat to peace?"

The men pulled Gordon and Sherman apart. Sherman's nose was bleeding. They dusted themselves off and strode off in different directions. Gordon went around the corner of the house. Sherman got into a BMW and drove off, wheels squealing. Even his car was yuppie. Corn bread aristocracy.

Then I felt Jon's arms around me in a sudden hug. "Let's get out of here," he said.

We went to the Port City Chop House to celebrate. "First thing in the morning we'll draw up new plans," I said. "We'll make that house beautiful."

"Will you forgive me if I say I'm glad someone polished off Mirabelle?" he asked.

THIRTY-ONE

"ASHLEY, YOU'VE GOT to help me with this house," Melanie cried over the phone. "You're the only one who can decide which of these antiques will go to Campbell House and which we should offer to local dealers."

As usual when Melanie is excited I don't know what she's talking about. "What house? What antiques?"

"I thought I told you. Mirabelle's lawyers want me to put her Landfall house on the market right away so they can settle her estate."

"Wait a minute! Mirabelle's lawyers gave you the listing? Aren't those the same guys who were about to sue you and have your license revoked?"

"Oh, pish-posh. You can't believe a word lawyers say. They'll say anything to win a case. They knew none of those accusations were true. But a contract, that's another matter. They know I'm the best. They've signed my listing agreement, six percent to me, and I can get a mil, at least 900 thou for this place. It's big. And fifteen percent of all the personal property I sell. So are you coming or not? You'd better because otherwise these antiques will go to the highest bidder."

I looked around at the mess in my own house. Well, it would just have to wait. How like Melanie to ask for my help without offering to help me! But antiques! Mirabelle had some nice things.

It took me all of five minutes to reach her house. Melanie was waiting at the front door. "OK, look around, put these tags on what you want. Here come the packers. You'd better get moving."

"I'll have all Mirabelle's kitchen stuff moved out of Campbell House so there will be room to store these antiques until I figure out what goes where," I said. So many good things were happening.

She went out in the driveway to speak to the guy who was rolling down the truck's rear door, and I headed for the dining room where a Sheraton breakfront beckoned to me. The entire house was done in non-colors, pale creams and off-whites so that the antiques and art stood out. I moved from room to room, hanging bright red tags on the pieces the storage people were not to touch.

I opened a door in the living room to discover a tiny office/computer station. The computer was gone. The police, I assumed, had taken it. I slid open a file drawer. Red file folders. Most of the files were missing, but a few remained, obviously of no interest to the police.

In the meantime, the crew carried in boxes, large rolls of bubble wrap, enough tape guns to wrap the city, and went to work upstairs, packing up the bedrooms.

"Ashley?" Melanie called from the stairs.

I closed the computer workstation door. "In here," I answered.

She appeared in the doorway. Light streaming in from the open front door struck her hair, turning it to the orange that is known as Titian red. Another beautiful outfit in muted greens. And I in my jeans and sweatshirt. Would I never learn?

"I'm just going to run over to the next street to show a house. I won't be gone more than thirty minutes. Keep an eye on those fools upstairs, will you? I don't want any sticky fingers lifting things we can sell."

I shrugged. "Sure, I'll hang around."

The minute she was out the door, I was back inside the miniature office. Why hadn't the police taken all her papers? Obviously, some things were of interest, like, for instance, the papers for the loan Gordon Cushman had made to Mirabelle. Not a trace of it.

I thumbed through the remaining folders. One contained employment records for those who had worked on *Southern Style.* King's resume, agreements with the union, letters of reference. Apparently, Mirabelle had acted as her own producer. There were records for a half dozen technicians, although none of their names rang a bell. Teddy Lambston's employment records too, a resume, his transcript from NYU, a recommendation letter from the station manager at WUNC-TV. And Mirabelle's brokerage statements. Hieroglyphics. The numbers meant nothing to me, the only thing I recognized was Sherman Warner's name.

Whoa! What did I just see? An employment application from Muffie Warner, with a hand-written note clipped to it saying that Muffie's pageant experience had prepared her for a guest spot on *Southern Style*. She could do photographic essays. Several sample photos of historic downtown houses were included, one of them Campbell House.

I grabbed up the files, carried them out to my car which was parked in the street, pushed them under the front seat and locked the car. Then I went back inside the house, as innocent as you please, to babysit the packers till their mama came home. While I waited I flipped through Mirabelle's photo albums. One picture brought me up short: Daddy with Reggie and Shelby and Mirabelle. It looked like a party. Shelby had her arm linked through Daddy's.

THIRTY-TWO

ON SATURDAY EVENING, Melanie led the way into the Northeast Library. We were both wearing Halloween masks, the black bandit kind, and it was hard to see with my peripheral vision blocked. I always did love dressing up in costumes but the idea of attending the Cape Fear Crime Festival's Halloween party had been Melanie's and she'd bought our tickets. "It'll be fun," she'd said when she invited me. "Like when we were kids. Remember?"

Who could forget the excitement of Halloween when you were a kid? Being out after dark, other kids you saw every day now unrecognizable in their masks and costumes, the thrill of feeling unknown behind your own mask.

Melanie was dressed up like Cleopatra, a long black straight wig with bangs under a golden tiara that was shaped like a coiled snake about to strike. Luckily it was another warm, humid evening because all she had on was a gold bra and a long linen wrap skirt. Snake bracelets adorned her upper arms and bejeweled flip-flops slapped the bottoms of her bare feet as we crossed the crowded parking lot.

At the door to the large meeting room we were

welcomed by Nicki Leone, a founder and board member of the mystery writers' conference. Nicki was dressed as Morticia Addams in a long slinky black dress with sleeves that fluttered at her wrists. Her dark hair, normally pinned up in a knot, flowed to her waist in waves.

The room was overflowing with guests in costume and masks. There were cowboys and cowgirls, a magician with a black cape, wand, and top hat, Southern belles, witches with pointy hats.

The festival was an annual event, held around Halloween, that attracts three to five hundred mystery writers and fans from as far away as St. Bart's and Canada.

The large room was cleverly decorated with tombstones and bales of hay, spiders dangling from silken webs, black cats, pumpkins, and even an improvised coffin.

"Would you like to buy a raffle ticket?" Detective Ed Gibson of Wilmington P.D. asked. "The proceeds go to the Guardian ad Litem program for abused and neglected children," he explained. "Last year we raised $1,700. It's for a good cause. Six tickets for five dollars." He offered a basket of tickets.

I reached into the pocket of the baggy clown suit I'd rented and pulled out a ten and gave it to him. Melanie's costume was so skimpy I assumed she wasn't carrying any money, unless she'd tucked a twenty in her bra. I turned to hand her six tickets but she was gone. I looked around and spotted her nearby, talking to Dorothy Hodder of the New Hanover County Library, another of the board members. For tonight Dorothy was Scarlett, and I wished Mama could have seen her. She had on a scarlet gown trimmed with black lace, a black feather boa, and a hat with black ostrich plumes.

I was served a glass of wine which I carried as I strolled to the tables where the gift baskets for the raffle drawing were displayed. Books by festival authors were offered along with paintings and gift items. The baskets were attractive, and very desirable. I didn't know which I wanted most, so I distributed my tickets among them.

Melanie sidled up next to me. "You won't believe what she's been telling everyone."

"What who's been telling everyone?" I asked, folding my last ticket and sliding it into the appropriate slot.

"Cecily. She's the keynote speaker."

I looked at her. "I didn't know that. You paid good money to hear Cecily Cushman speak. I think I've heard it all."

"You haven't heard this! She's told everyone she's going to name the killer in her speech tonight! Can you believe that? What could she possibly know? It's just a publicity stunt to sell more books."

I gave Melanie a serious look. "That wasn't a smart thing for her to do."

We worked our way around the room, checking out the placement of dinner tables, deciding where we wanted to sit. Each table was assigned to an author, and that person's book was centered on the table. In the next room, the caterers were getting organized to serve dinner, and even over the din of loud voices I could hear the sounds of chopping, slicing, dicing, and the occasional bang of a pot.

"Oh, look, here's *Circle of Secrets,* Dixie Land's latest book. I just love her name; it's real, you know. Let's sit here."

A magician in a long black cloak pushed past me rudely. "Well, pardon you," I called indignantly to his retreating back. Some people!

"Wait a minute," Melanie called from the next table, "what about Dorothy O'Neill? Here's her latest book. *Grim Finale.* I know it will be good."

I smiled, really getting into the spirit of the festival now. "I told you this would be fun," Melanie said.

I moved forward for a closer look at O'Neill's book: deep red comedy and tragedy masks centered on the cover. Next to the table, up against the wall, was an improvised coffin, black with massive spider webs and a huge looming spider. Raggedy Anne was lying in the coffin, her blue gingham skirt hiked up, her long red and white striped legs splayed. Her head was kind of droopy like she was taking a nap. Or was she drunk? An overturned wine glass lay near the coffin. I moved closer, intending to pick up the glass thinking that if someone stepped on it there'd be dangerous glass slivers.

My clown shoes were big and clumsy and I felt my foot slip on the spilled wine. I flung out my arms to get my balance but was falling anyway.

I was falling into the coffin, aiming straight for Raggedy Anne. I threw out a hand to break my fall and snagged her orange yarn wig. Then I was lying beside her, face to face, her wig in my hand. Long strands of pure white hair spilled over her pale face. Even with the painted-on freckles and spots of red color on her cheeks I identified Cecily Cushman.

A crowd had gathered around us. "Let me help you up," a man in a cowboy outfit offered, reaching for my hand.

"Are you OK?" Melanie asked at the same time.

I gave him my hand and let him help me to my feet. "Something's wrong with Cecily!" I shouted. She hadn't even flinched when I'd fallen into her. "She's not moving!"

The cowboy knelt and shook her shoulder. "Cecily?"

Raggedy Anne rolled onto her side. The brown wooden handle of a butcher's knife protruded from her back.

"Oh, no! Not again!" I cried.

THIRTY-THREE

I SLEPT LATE ON SUNDAY morning. My sleep had been plagued by nightmares until early morning. Today I was just going to take it easy. Sunday, the day of rest. There'd been way too much excitement in my life recently.

Melanie was probably working in her office, catching up on paper work until it was time to show houses. Jon had told me he'd be working at home, finalizing the new drawings for changes we were making in Campbell House.

I dressed casually, took the Sunday *Star-News* and drove over to Harbour Island for breakfast at the Causeway Cafe. After I gorged myself on eggs and grits and an eyeful of news about how Ashley Wilkes, historic preservationist, had literally stumbled upon another dead body, I drove home to find my dog-walking neighbor standing in front of my house. He had an umbrella and a friendly collie with a thick coat. I stepped under his umbrella when he motioned to me.

"I've been keeping an eye on your house when your car is gone."

"Well, thanks," I said. "But I've got a burglar alarm now. That should help."

"You had a gentleman caller while you were out," he informed me.

"Oh?"

"He stood up on your front porch for quite a while. Then he left."

"What did he look like?" Nick? I wondered.

"Couldn't see much of him. He was under an umbrella. Thought you'd like to know. We've got to look out for each other."

"You're right," I said. "And thanks."

I unlocked my door and turned off the alarm, looking for a note from my visitor. None. The day was pleasantly cool with a light drizzle. My ferns were flourishing in all the humidity. I left the door standing open and sat out in my swing with the paper.

But I couldn't concentrate to read. Instead, I kept seeing Cecily's dead face as she lay beside me in the coffin. Detective Ed Gibson had pushed through the crowd to kneel beside Cecily. "She's dead," he'd declared. He called for a homicide unit. Then he'd instructed Phyllis Smith, the manager of the Northwest Branch, to lock all the exits. No one was to leave.

"It's too late," I'd told him. "It was the magician. And he's gone."

Whoever he was, he thought Cecily was about to expose him. Did she really know the identity of Mirabelle's killer? She'd been questioning everyone. Maybe she had learned something. But if so, wouldn't she have saved that information for her new book? And wasn't she obligated to tell the police?

I went inside and did some laundry, cleaned the bathroom, dusted, devoted my energies to activities that produced results. After three calls from reporters, I turned off the ringer on the telephone. It was nice being alone, being quiet.

At about six, I fixed a sandwich and a glass of iced tea and carried a tray back out to the porch. The sky was black now. Coin-sized raindrops plopped on the railings and bushes. The steady downpour obliterated all other noises. With the gentle sway of the swing, I almost nodded off right there, but worrisome questions chased around in my brain.

What did it mean that Daddy had been photographed with Shelby, Reggie, and Mirabelle? He knew them, of course. Daddy knew everybody. But he wasn't a ladies' man. In fact, he was shy around women and treated them with old-fashioned courtliness. With Mama he'd always been sweetly affectionate, treating her like she was fragile. Which she was.

Whatever Daddy's association with them, it had to be innocent. Probably just a political function, I assured myself. But Shelby had looked so smug in that photo, her arm linked through his like she owned him.

Hold on a sec. Bob King told me he and Daddy had been friends. Maybe the person behind the camera was King. Maybe there was a connection.

"No more!" I cried aloud. I got up and went inside, rinsed my dishes and stacked them in the dishwasher. Then I closed and locked the doors and windows and turned on the burglar alarm. The moment my head hit the pillow I dropped into a troubled sleep.

I don't know how long I slept but I awoke disoriented. What time was it? Darkness and heavy rain pressed against the windows. I had slept away the evening. The digits on my clock blinked. While I slept there'd been a power interruption. Turning on the lights, I tried to remember my dream. Something important was niggling at my brain. A clue. But what was it? I went for my stash of evidence, pulled Mirabelle's red file folders off my closet shelf and dumped them on the bed.

"The answer's here, somewhere," I said aloud, opening the files at random. I withdrew a document from the file, then stared at it, incredulous. Idiot! Why hadn't I noticed this discrepancy before?

Now Nick would have to listen to me. I picked up the phone to call him but there was somebody on the line.

Wind rattled the shutters and rain pounded the windowpanes noisily making it hard to hear the voice on the other end. "Ashley?"

"Melanie? Is that you?"

"Ashley, you've got to come. He's got a gun and he'll kill me."

"Melanie! Where are you? What's going on?"

"Shut up, Ashley, and listen! Did you take some files from Mirabelle's?" Melanie's voice drifted away, she was talking to him. I heard the rumble of a man's voice in the background. Then she said, "He says you have them. You've got to bring them."

"Yes, but…"

"Bring them to Campbell House. And don't call the police. If you do, he'll kill me. Hurry, I…"

There was a click. "Melanie? Melanie?" I cried into the dead phone.

In no time I pulled on jeans and sneakers, a sweat shirt, and a yellow rubber raincoat. I stuffed the file folders into the raincoat's inside pocket. Grabbing my purse and car keys, I bolted off the porch and dashed through the downpour to my car.

Backing the car out onto Summer Rest Road, I shot out to Eastwood Road. Even with my windshield wipers set high, I couldn't see the markers on the road through the heavy wash of rain. I passed few cars as I tore out Oleander toward town, not bothering to stop for the red lights that bobbed perilously on swinging cables. Powerful winds lashed the trees. A trash barrel rolled out into the street and glanced off my right front fender. I kept going.

Someone was holding Melanie at gun point, and I knew just who he was. He'd broken into my house, looking for the key to the Campbells' front door. He must have been watching me and seen me put Mirabelle's file folders into my car. Now he was using Melanie to get to me. He knows I know he's killed before and that he'll kill again if he has to.

I'd do anything to save her. I just hoped I'd be able to talk him into letting us go once he had the evidence. I didn't dare call Nick. A cornered killer had nothing to lose. He'd shoot Melanie!

I snapped on the radio for news of the storm. Hurricane Nancy was headed for the Outer Banks, a hyper newscaster reported. Wilmington would be spared a direct hit, but a deluge of rain would be dumped on the city and massive flooding was expected. Storm surge, almost as dangerous as a hurricane. Then the mayor came on, asking for calm, reminding us that Wilmingtonians never evacuate for we are seasoned survivors of storms.

At Seventeenth Street I made a right, then turned left into Orange Street, sped to Campbell House and skidded to a stop so fast I ran up on the curb.

I battled stiff winds to get my car door open, then dashed through the heavy rain up the sidewalk. The house lay in darkness, as still as death. I paused a minute under the magnolia trees. Their leaves were so dense they sheltered me from the downpour, but easterly winds blew rain sideways into my face and soaked my hair.

I shook with fright. I was about to confront a killer but couldn't avoid it. Melanie was in danger. She'd do the same for me. I had to be strong. I crept onto the portico. The front door was open a crack. Cautiously, I pushed it open.

"Melanie?" I called softly.

When she didn't answer, I shouted, "Melanie, where are you?"

"Back here," a muffled voice called from the rear of the house.

I made my way down the hall, feeling along the cold wall. In my haste I'd forgotten to bring a flashlight.

Parting the vinyl sheets, I groped my way into the

kitchen area. In the darkness, rubble under my sneakers felt like boulders and I struggled not to stumble.

"Melanie?" I called in a loud whisper.

THIRTY-FOUR

"ASHLEY!" HER VOICE drifted out of the darkness. "Did you bring the files?"

"Yes, I've got them."

Instantly a match was struck, a candle glowed. In its flickering light, I saw my sister's face and darted toward her. She was tied to a straight back chair. Standing over her with a gun pointed at her head was Teddy Lambston.

"Oh, Teddy, how could you? I thought we were friends."

He was dressed in the suit he'd worn to the funeral. His hair was wet and slicked back in a pony tail. At his feet lay a large duffel bag. In the candlelight, his eyes were black hollows. "I don't have any friends. Do you think I'm stupid? I know the names you all called me in school."

I took a step forward. "Not me, Teddy. I never called you names. We were friends."

"Don't come any closer." I'd never heard him speak so assertively before. I stopped and he said, "OK, very slowly, put the files on the floor."

I reached inside my raincoat.

"Stop!" Teddy yelled. The gun swung from Melanie to me.

I held my hands out. "I'm not armed, Teddy. The folders are inside my raincoat."

He waved the gun at me. "Use both hands and open your raincoat wide so I can see inside."

I pulled back my slicker.

"Remove the files and set them on the floor."

I stooped and laid three folders on the floor. As I straightened up I peered into Melanie's face to see how she was holding up. She looked furious. "Are you all right?" I asked.

She wiggled in the chair, trying to pull loose. "He's had me tied up all day. This sociopath lured me over to his house with a phony story about having me do an appraisal." Her chin shot up and she fixed Teddy with an angry glare. "Then after dark he marched me over here at gun point."

Teddy kicked Melanie's chair and she squealed. "Shut up!" he yelled.

I took another step closer to her, hoping he wouldn't notice. How was I going to untie her? "Teddy, let us go. You've got what you want." I played dumb. "There's nothing in them to incriminate you so why are you doing this?"

"You're lying, Ashley."

A flash of memory danced before my eyes. Maybe it was seeing Teddy in candlelight that brought the memory back. On the night of the Campbells' last Christmas party, when I'd gone into Shelby's bedroom to fetch Mama's coat, Shelby had been standing inside one of the tall windows with one other person. There had been candles burning on a dresser. The couple had sprung apart and looked so guilty when I saw them, I'd shared their embarrassment, and that's why I'd blocked the memory. Until now.

"You were in love with Shelby! But you were only eighteen, Teddy! She was close to thirty."

"Don't you dare say a word against her," he warned, his words cold and clipped. I'd never seen Teddy like this.

"Shelby was perfect, in every way. She was the only person besides my mother who loved me. She and Reggie. They were the only friends I had. They were good to me. We had fun together. The kids in high school all treated me like a freak. The guys called me 'Sissie.' The girls accepted me as one of them but ridiculed me behind my back. Do you think I didn't know what went on?

"Then Shelby and Reggie befriended me, and it was like they held up a mirror for me—a magic mirror in which I was everything I dreamed of being. They...they cared about me."

Melanie screeched, "Oh, please, spare me the hearts and flowers. You've got what you want. Now untie me! My arms are numb."

"If you loved them so much, why did you kill them?" I asked.

Teddy became distracted. His eyes flitted about, sweat glistened on his upper lip. Maybe it wasn't hopeless; maybe I could get the gun away from him. Or untie Melanie so we could make a run for it. Moving cautiously, I sidled closer to her. She eyed me intently. Read my mind. Kept her mouth shut.

"You've got it wrong," Teddy cried. Tears rolled down his cheeks. "I'm not a killer. Not unless I'm forced to, like Mirabelle forced me. And that awful Cecily, threatening to expose me. But Mother killed Reggie and Shelby. She found the three of us together one night. Mother was very possessive. Until Shelby and Reggie, it had just been the two of us. My dad abandoned us when I was a baby."

"But I thought your father was dead." I took another step toward Melanie.

"That's what we wanted everyone to think," Teddy said dreamily.

I had to keep him talking. "Deborah found the three of you in...the bedroom?" Poor Teddy. I almost felt sorry for him.

Teddy laughed hysterically. The tears on his cheeks shone in the candlelight. "Mother said they had corrupted me. She forbade me to ever see them again. She insisted they leave me alone, but they refused. So did I. She didn't understand."

"And she killed them to protect you," I said sympathetically.

Teddy seemed not to hear, lost in memories of that terrible night. "Why did she have to interfere? The three of us were happy together. I hate her. I'm glad she's dead."

"You don't mean that," I said, trying to soothe him. I recalled the bullet hole in the bedroom door frame. "She shot Reggie, didn't she? She was trying to protect you."

"She must have crept up the stairs that night. She had a gun. I didn't know she owned one. Reggie tried to reason with her. One minute he was talking calmly to her and reaching out to take the gun. The next minute the gun exploded. Mother shot wildly, out of control. Reggie raised his arms to cover his head, and the bullets struck him in the chest. One of them must have hit his heart. He fell. I couldn't save him."

Teddy was sobbing now and I seized the opportunity to move closer to Melanie. "At least, he didn't suffer," Teddy gulped. "Not like my darling Shelby."

"Shelby ran," I guessed.

"Poor Shelby. She was so scared. Mother was waving this gun at her. She took off. Ran out of the room. Mother shot after her but missed. Then we heard an awful thud. There was no mistaking that sound. Shelby fell down the stairs. I ran after her but I was too late to save her." Teddy raised his free hand to his forehead, covering his eyes as if to blot out the memory.

One more step and I'd be able to reach the rope.

Melanie's eyes were huge, she seemed to be holding her breath.

"Shelby's death was an accident," I said soothingly, hoping to keep him distracted.

"Oh, jeez. Oh, jeez." Teddy doubled over, clutching his stomach. The gun pointed at the floor. "Stop it! Stop talking about it. I can't take any more." He looked straight at me.

Poor Teddy. What a tormented soul. But I couldn't let myself feel pity now. I had to use his grief against him. Use it to free us.

Yet Teddy seemed unable to stop talking. Probably,

this was his first opportunity to confess the terrible events of that night. "She made me put their bodies in the wall. Mother made me. She was very clever. She made me put on Reggie's clothes, and she put on Shelby's. We pulled hats over our faces and carried suit-cases out to the car. Old lady Burns used to prowl around at night. Mother felt sure she'd see us. Then she'd tell everyone she'd seen Reggie and Shelby leave town."

"What did you do with the car?" I asked. Teddy was sitting on the floor, his knees drawn up to his chin. The gun dangled loosely in his hand. I reached behind Melanie and began working on the knots.

"We drove to the airport and left it in long-term parking. When it was found, it supported the story that Shelby and Reggie had flown to Europe. We checked into a hotel near the airport for the night. Mother didn't want anyone here to see us return to our house that night. The next day, we took a cab to the river, then walked home as if we'd been down at the waterfront."

The rope was slackening.

"Stop that!" Teddy yelled. "Get your hands away from her!" He lunged to his feet, waved the gun wildly at me, probably as crazily as his mother had waved it at Shelby on another October night in this very house six years ago.

"Oh, my God! He's going to kill us," Melanie squealed. "We're going to die!"

THIRTY-FIVE

I RAISED MY PALMS and backed off. "Just satisfy my curiosity about one thing, Teddy." I prayed for a miracle, divine inspiration that would enable me to save myself and Melanie. "Why did you kill Mirabelle?"

Teddy was staggering, openly sobbing, and waving the gun threateningly. "I'm not a killer by choice. I'm not an evil person. I never wanted to kill anyone or to see anyone die. I hated putting Reggie and Shelby in that wall. I loved them. But that Mirabelle…"

"She was blackmailing you, wasn't she?" I guessed.

"Yes. She was evil. She was going to tell if I didn't give her my house. The only thing I had left or cared about."

"So you never meant to sell it!" Melanie huffed.

Now that Teddy was confessing, his words tumbled out as if he had no control over them. "I'd never sell. But Mirabelle threatened me that if I didn't sign it over to her, she'd tell the police I was in Wilmington that October when Reggie and Shelby were murdered, instead of at NYU like I told Detective Yost. She'd give them the key. Then they'd have been suspicious of me, and started nosing around."

I kept my voice neutral when I said, "But you didn't

start college until January." That's what I had seen on his college transcript.

Teddy seemed to sag momentarily, to shrink. "I was stupid to ever give that transcript to Mirabelle! Naturally Miss Busybody Morgan picked up on it right away. Then she came over to my house, acting just so sweet, and I was so lonely I thought she was my friend. When I went out to the kitchen to make us iced tea, she must have snooped around in Mother's room and found the key to Campbell House there."

I nodded sympathetically.

Teddy seemed to be talking to himself. "I'd never given that key a second thought. But Mirabelle recognized that large brass key immediately and knew what it meant. She took it and tried it in the door. When it fit the lock, she brought it back and waved it under my nose. That's when she blackmailed me."

Teddy's eyes were filled with pain. "She was a monster. I did the world a favor by getting rid of her. Besides if I hadn't killed her, someone else would have. Everyone hated her."

"You're right on that score," Melanie said. I'd succeeded in loosening her bonds. She was twisting her wrists in the ropes.

Teddy chuckled. "Yeah." He looked at Melanie with admiration.

She pleaded, "Teddy, please untie me."

"Yeah," Teddy said again, not looking at either of us, "everybody hated her." He bent down to stuff the file folders into his duffel bag. Outside thunder crashed with a bang. He jumped. He looked insane. His eyes flashed around the room desperately. "I've got to get out of town for a while."

"Will you go back to New York?" I asked, hoping to encourage him to get on his way.

"Yes. A person can lose himself in New York if he knows how. I do. I never should have left."

Melanie's hands were almost free.

Teddy rambled, needing to be understood. "That's where Mother took me after she killed Reggie and Shelby. She left me with an antique dealer friend of hers while she went to London on a buying trip. Just like nothing had happened. As if she hadn't just killed the two dearest people in the world to me.

"It took me a long time to get over the tragedy of that night. Eventually I did. I discovered people like myself in New York. I made friends. I was happy there. Then Mother died and I inherited our house. It was the one thing I cherished. I wanted to live in it again. You saw for yourself, Ashley, how I was fixing it up."

"Yes, Teddy, and you were doing a splendid job. Your mother would have liked what you were doing. She paid the property taxes on Campbell House, didn't she? And sent those postcards?"

"I didn't know until you found Reggie and Shelby, and everything came out, that Mother had been paying their property taxes while she was alive. If I'd known, I would have found a way to continue paying them. I'd never even thought about property taxes and that if they weren't paid, the City would sell the house.

Mother was always smart. She said Reggie and Shelby didn't ever have to leave their home." The dreamy look returned. "I always liked knowing they were close by."

He was really disturbed. The loneliness of his childhood combined with his rejection as an adolescent, then falling in love with Reggie and Shelby and seeing them die—all that trauma had sent him over the edge.

He shook his head as if to clear it. "All right," he said with determination, "time to get this show on the road. Ashley, you untie Melanie."

"It's about time," Melanie said.

Somehow I didn't think it was going to be as simple as that. "He's not going to let us go," I whispered as I pulled the ropes free. "If you get a chance, run for it."

"Stop that whispering!" Teddy yelled. With the gun in one hand, and the candle in the other, he motioned us out into the hall. "Open the basement door," he told me. He set the candle holder on the floor. The flame flickered.

What if I kick it over? I wondered. Would it go out? In the darkness, we could escape.

"Wait a minute," Melanie protested. "We're not going down there. There's a hurricane coming."

Teddy laughed cynically. "Ashley, I'll bet you've got it figured out. Tell her what's going to happen."

Melanie looked stunned. "What? What's going to happen?"

"Get hold of yourself," I said. "I need you to be steady. Teddy's got the only evidence against him now. He'll destroy it. That means that we are his only threat. The police don't suspect him. There's no reason for them to check his NYU record. They think you did it, Melanie."

"And with you two dead, within a reasonable length of time I can come home again and finish decorating my house," Teddy said.

"With all this rain, the basement could flood!" Melanie screeched. "Well, you're not locking me down there." She plunged past him, but he caught her arm and threw her to the floor.

"You're not going anywhere!" He yanked the basement door open and snapped on the lights. The power was on.

"Don't make me shoot you! Get down there now!"

"No!" Melanie screamed.

Teddy grabbed her wrist and dragged her to the stairs, then pushed. I saw my chance to run for the front door, to flee, maybe find help. But I couldn't let Melanie face that basement alone. I scrambled down the steps behind her and caught her. She was thrashing, trying to keep her balance as she slid down the steep flight of stairs. With my arms wrapped around her, we slipped and tumbled to the bottom.

I looked back up the stairs just as Teddy slammed the door shut. The key turned in the lock. We were locked in. Seconds later I felt wind blow through the house as Teddy opened the front door. It banged shut behind him.

"Are you all right?"

"I think so. My backside is sore, but I don't think anything's broken. How about you?"

"I'm OK. We've got to find a way out of here."

"We're going to die," she wailed. "And there are spiders. My arms are numb. That fruitcake had me tied up all day."

"I'm sorry," I said, rubbing her wrists.

"You should be. This is all your fault. If you hadn't taken those files, none of this would have happened."

THIRTY-SIX

"WHO WOULD HAVE ever thought? Deborah Lambston! I can't believe it," Melanie said.

We were sitting on the steps, trying to figure a way out. "She did make a lot of buying trips to Europe. She sent postcards and letters from all over Europe and signed them Shelby Campbell."

"Are you sure there's not one window down here that's not boarded up?" Melanie asked for the umpteenth time.

"I saw them all from the outside. They're sealed. And they're so high up, we couldn't reach them anyway. We've already looked twice."

Even from the depths of the solid basement, we could hear the force of the storm smashing overhead.

"We'll just wait it out," I said.

"What's that?" she asked hysterically.

I looked where she pointed. A silent stream of water came rolling up to the bottom of the steps. "Oh, no! Storm surge."

The water came pouring in, rising fast. I pointed to the chalky line on the wall. "That's how high the water rose the last time there was a flood. If we sit up on that top step, we'll be fine. Our heads will be above water."

"But how do we know the water won't rise higher this time? All the way to the first floor. We'll drown. Oh, no, look." She pointed. A rat was swimming toward our feet, trying not to drown, wanting to climb the stairs.

We kicked at him and he swam into a corner.

Melanie ran up the stairs. "That does it. I'm getting out of here." She banged on the door and threw her shoulder against it but it wouldn't budge.

I jumped off the stairs and splashed in the knee-deep water toward one of the storage rooms with Melanie yelling after me, "Are you crazy? Where are you going?"

"I'm not going to just sit here and wait until the water's up over our heads."

I remembered that I'd seen some tools in one of the cabinets in the scullery. Flinging open cabinet doors, I found what I was looking for, a screw driver with a bright red handle. Dashing back to the steps, I mounted them two at a time. "Move aside. Maybe I can get that lock open."

Melanie stood close behind me, nudging my back. "Help! Somebody help us!" she screamed.

An especially loud thunderbolt crashed near the house. The lights flickered, wavered, then died. The basement was thrown into pitch blackness.

We screamed together. Then, like a miracle, the lights blinked back on again. "Dear lord, let them hold," I breathed.

I inserted the blade of the screwdriver between the door and the jamb. The lock's plate fit flush on the left edge of the door. The lock was simple, an old-fashioned spring lock with a bolt that slid out of the plate into a reciprocal chamber carved in the door jamb. That's where I attacked.

"Hurry up," Melanie screeched. "The water's getting higher." Her hysteria was contagious.

"Stop pushing," I snapped. "And keep quiet so I can concentrate."

The lights flashed, died. I groaned. Sliding the screwdriver up and down, I felt when it hit the bolt. Tilting the screwdriver, I wedged its tip inside the chamber and under the bolt. I almost had it when the door suddenly flew open. A flash of lightning revealed an old woman holding the door open, motioning for me to step through.

I scrambled out of the basement. Melanie hurried behind me.

"Oh, thank goodness, you got us out of there," she cried.

"I didn't. An old woman opened the door."

"Who? That old woman who lives across the street? Where did she go? She isn't here now. Come on. Let's see how bad it is outside. Maybe we can leave."

She opened the front door a crack while I remained behind, looking around. I knew who I'd seen. And it wasn't Ellen Burns.

We peered out into the storm. The big magnolias were holding their own but limbs and thick leaves thrashed. Smaller trees were down. Water flooded the sidewalk and street and was rising up around my car. The wind tore through the trees, battering the house.

"I think we'd better wait upstairs. This house is solid.

There's a balcony off the master bedroom, we can watch the storm from there."

With only lightning flashes to light our way, we climbed the stairs, moved past the ballroom, then down the hall and into Shelby's bedroom. I jerked open the French doors onto the balcony at the rear of the house.

"We'll get wet," Melanie shouted. "Oh, shoot, where's my brain? My cell phone's in my purse downstairs. I'll get it. We'll call for help."

Without warning she threw her arms around me and hugged me tight. "Listen, baby sister, I just want to tell you, you are the bravest thing. I had a hand in raising you, so I'm going to take some of the credit."

"Brave?" I asked, not trusting my ears.

"'Course you're brave. Went to New York City when you were only eighteen. Found yourself a nice roommate. Got your degree. I didn't have the nerve to do something like that. And you were wonderful with Teddy. And you…you got us out of that basement. I was too flustered to think. Now let me go get my phone before you start me bawling."

I shook my head. What could you do with a sister like Melanie but love her?

"Let's see if we can find some candles and matches," I said. A lightning flash revealed candles in candlesticks on the dresser. Rummaging through the drawers, I found matches. But would they be any good after six years? I struck a few with no luck, then one ignited. I lit two candles, one for the room, and one for Melanie to carry back down the stairs.

"Take off those high heels. I don't want you falling down those stairs like Shelby did."

Melanie kicked off her shoes then disappeared down the hall, a wavering light that got smaller and smaller. "Hold on to the banister!" I yelled after her.

I saw then how Melanie and I had changed. How I'd changed. All my life I'd been longing for her approval. Now I had it. And something more. We were equals. Finally, I'd caught up to her. From now on our relationship would be better, give and take, mutual respect. I didn't have to walk in her shadow any longer.

Some minutes later she returned with the phone and I was surprised when we got through to 911. "Tell them to call Nick Yost and tell him that Teddy Lambston is the murderer and that he's getting away," I instructed. The dispatcher assured us we would be rescued, but as we were in no imminent danger, it might take a while. The police and rescue squads had their hands full, he said, but he promised to get our message to Detective Yost.

"OK, let's try to make ourselves comfortable," Melanie suggested. She jerked down the satin coverlet on Shelby's bed and plumped up the pillows, releasing six years of dust. I coughed.

"Come on," she coaxed. "Get in. I'm so dirty a little dust won't hurt. This is kind of cozy with the candlelight and all."

It was kind of cozy, like when we were kids and got under the covers with our flashlights. "OK, big sister, now you're trapped. You have to answer me. How did the brooch get inside Shelby's sofa?"

"All right. I'll tell you. But I'm breaking my promise to Mama."

"She won't know."

"Sure enough. OK, well, six years ago after you went off to New York, Daddy started acting pretty peculiar. In hindsight I think he was just missing you. Mama got it in her head that he was having an affair with Shelby Campbell because of some photograph she'd seen with Daddy and Shelby together in it. Mama insisted that she was going to confront Shelby and I couldn't let her go alone. So we came here. Mama was wearing the brooch and it must have fallen off and got lodged down behind the seat cushion where it's been hidden for all these years."

I took a deep breath. I had to ask the next question. "And was Daddy having an affair with Shelby?"

Melanie waved a hand. "No way. Shelby laughed her head off at us. Thought we were a couple of fools. I never was so embarrassed. She said Daddy was a prude. Can you believe it? The photo was taken at some political fund-raiser. Mama just went haywire. She always was different."

I hugged a dusty pillow. "Between the two of them, it's a wonder we're not as crazy as loons."

Melanie giggled. "We're Southerners, we're supposed to be crazy."

"So Daddy's accident really was an accident?" I asked timidly.

Melanie put her arm around me. "Poor baby sister. Have you been worrying about that all these years? Yes, it really was an accident. A witness said a golden retriever ran into the road and Daddy swerved trying to avoid hitting it and hit a tree instead. He might have saved himself if he hadn't tried to save the dog."

"A dog? Oh, lord, why didn't anyone tell me?"

"I thought you knew. Poor Ashley, up there in New York all by yourself, worrying about this."

We were quiet for a moment. Then she said, "Mama missed you so much when you went to New York. You were her baby. She loved you best."

I couldn't believe my ears. "But I always thought she loved you best, Mel."

"No, we were too much alike. After you left home, she sat me down one day and told me how special you were. She said how she'd never expected to have a second baby but when you came along, she fell in love with you. You were so sweet, always trying to please everyone. She said when she was gone I should take care of you, that we should take care of each other. I think she knew something was happening to her mind and she was preparing me."

A loud thump hit the house. Another tree limb down.

"We do take care of each other, big sis," I said.

"Sure 'nuff, baby sis." We hugged.

Another loud thud. "Someone's banging on the door," I whispered, alarmed.

"It better not be that looney-tunes Teddy," she said.

"No way is he getting in here. Come on." Carrying the candle, I lead the way down the stairs, crossed the hall, and peered out through the sidelight.

With a cry, I flung open the door. He stepped inside,

reaching for me, and I flew into his arms. He held me tight, one hand caressing my hair. "Thank God you're safe," Nick said. "I got your message and came right away."

Only then did I realize how wet he was, water dripping from his hair and his bright orange slicker. I didn't care. I hugged him tighter.

"Did you get him?" I asked.

"The guys are looking for him. He won't get far in this storm."

His eyes searched mine. "Oh, God, Ashley I was so worried about you. If you'd been hurt, well…I owe you an apology." Over my head, he said to Melanie, "You, too."

"Damned straight," Melanie retorted but grinned.

THIRTY-SEVEN

"NO WAY COULD LAMBSTON get far in those flooded streets," Nick said. "His car got stuck. My guys found him wading in water up to his thighs. He confessed to everything when they brought him in. He's being charged with two counts of murder and two counts of accessory to murder."

We were at Campbell House, Jon and I were sharing our plans for the mansion with Nick and Melanie. The sun was shining; the water had receded. Clean up crews were working to restore the shine to the Historic District. Christmas was coming and the annual candle-light tour of homes. All the bells and whistles had to be in perfect working order.

"Tell me something, Nick," I said, "what was Henry Cameron doing cruising my street the afternoon my house was broken into?"

"Just an innocent misunderstanding. He was looking for a house number and had the wrong address. Nothing sinister. We checked it out and the homeowner vouched for him."

"And what about Gordon and Sherman's fight? What was that about? I thought it might be an indication of guilt, crooks falling out."

"Warner did some investing for Cushman and lost a lot of money. Simple as that," Nick replied.

Jon asked, "How did Deborah Lambston know Henry Cameron, the caretaker?"

"Cameron had done some work for Mrs. Lambston. She knew he needed the money and wouldn't ask questions.

"And I can clear up another mystery for you. Lambston told us the murders affected his mother's mental stability. She became nocturnal, and often came here at night to play the organ."

"That's right!" I exclaimed. "She used to be a church organist before she went into decorating. But maybe we'd better keep this to ourselves. The tourists are really eating up Binkie's Ghost Walk tour." I thought of something else. "That also explains the missing wine."

"What missing wine?" Jon asked.

"The wine cellar was empty. Then, when I visited Teddy, he offered me wine from his mother's collection. She must have taken it to her house."

Nick took a deep breath and said, "Look, I've got some explaining to do and I'm not very good at this sort of thing so hear me out.

"Ashley, I was so worried that I'd be unduly influenced by our…ah, our friendship…that I failed to listen to you. It's one of the worst mistakes a detective can make. Melanie, I'm sorry you were accused, but at the time the evidence pointed to you."

He looked at me and smiled apologetically. Those dimples. He had the power to melt my resistance. But

I wasn't ready to let him know he was forgiven. Let him stew a little longer.

Melanie on the other hand was not the melting type. She gave Nick a withering glance from under her long lashes and said, "If my daddy was still alive, he'd have your job. You're lucky I don't sue you and the City."

"I'd like to make amends, starting by taking you both to dinner. I was wrong, I admit it."

"Thanks, but I'm having dinner with Joel. I think I've found the perfect property for his resort so we're celebrating."

"Ashley?" Nick asked.

"Well…" I began.

"Wait a minute," Jon interrupted. "I thought we agreed to take the dinner-dance cruise. They're back in business."

"Actually," I said, "I promised to meet Binkie." Looking out the window I saw him approaching the gate and went to meet him. Standing there in the mellow fall sunshine, I told him all about Teddy's confession and how he'd locked Melanie and me in the basement.

"Binkie, I saw Jean Campbell. She opened the door for us and let us out of the basement. Melanie never saw her. She thinks it was Ellen Burns. But it wasn't, it was Jean. Just telling you this gives me goose bumps."

He grinned. "So now you're a believer."

"How can I deny what I saw with my own eyes. Binkie, I've been giving this a lot of thought, trying to square the existence of spirits with my religious beliefs."

"And what did you decide?"

"Well, I'm a Christian. I was baptized at St. James, and

I try to attend regularly. So I believe that our soul belongs to God and that when we die our soul goes to God. Heaven and hell, just like we're taught in Sunday school.

"But I think that with some people, there's some bit of corporeal energy left behind. The human being is a complex creation. So some people have unfinished business, and with Jean Campbell, it was having her son and daughter-in-law murdered in her house, and hidden there. Some little part of her came back to grieve, to stay with them, to try to right the wrong. And she helped Melanie and me."

I looked at him and raised my eyebrows inquiringly. "What do you think?"

He put him arms around me and gave me a gentle squeeze. "I think you are the daughter I never had, Ashley dear. I'm proud of you."

The others came out on the portico. Melanie, the sister I admired and loved. Jon, my best bud. Nick, the man I was falling for.

I tossed a cheerful wave and smiled at them. Then I stepped through the gate.